The First Time Ever Published!

The Tenth Donut Mystery   OCT 2013

From *New York Times* Bestselling Author

Jessica Beck

DEADLY DONUTS

Books by Jessica Beck

The Donut Mysteries

Glazed Murder
Fatally Frosted
Sinister Sprinkles
Evil Éclairs
Tragic Toppings
Killer Crullers
Drop Dead Chocolate
Powdered Peril
Illegally Iced
Deadly Donuts

The Classic Diner Mysteries

A Chili Death
A Deadly Beef
A Killer Cake
A Baked Ham
A Bad Egg

The Ghost Cat Cozy Mysteries

Ghost Cat: Midnight Paws
Ghost Cat: Bid for Midnight

Jessica Beck is the *New York Times* Bestselling Author of
the
Donut Mysteries
as well as
The Classic Diner Mystery Series
and
The Ghost Cat Cozy Mysteries.

DEADLY DONUTS by Jessica Beck: Copyright © 2013

All rights reserved.

Recipes included in this book are to be recreated at the reader's own risk. The author is not responsible for any damage, medical or otherwise, created as a result of reproducing these recipes. It is the responsibility of the reader to ensure that none of the ingredients are detrimental to their health, and the author will not be held liable in any way for any problems that might arise from following the included recipes.

To my favorite cozy mystery writer in the world,
you know who you are!

Chapter 1

I'm not exactly proud of the fact that I slapped the stranger in Donut Hearts so hard across the cheek that his skin turned white, my handprint glowing on his face like a neon sign from the convenience store on the edge of town.

Part of it might have been because of the one-hundred-degree-plus heat wave we were experiencing on the first day of August in April Springs, North Carolina—bringing along with it plunging donut sales with every degree the temperature soared above ninety—and at least some of it had to be because of what the stranger had just said to me, but neither reason was a good excuse for the way I'd acted.

He was somewhere in his early forties, dressed in a suit that matched his jet-black hair, short of stature and yet stout in a way that made his powerful hands look oversized. I could easily imagine him squeezing someone's throat the way he was throttling the bag of donut holes in his hands, and there was an air about him that made me think he wouldn't react well to the physical abuse I'd unleashed on him.

To my credit, I *did* try to apologize. "I'm sorry. Don't get me wrong. I hate that you came in here trying to smear my father's memory, but I realize that hitting you like that was uncalled for." For the first time in days, I was glad that the donut shop was empty; no one had witnessed my outburst, though I suspected that Emma had heard the slap all the way back in the kitchen, even if she had her iPod cranked up to its highest level.

I expected the man to shout some kind of protest in reaction to my sharp slap, but instead, it merely deepened the smile he had already been showing. "I can understand your reaction, Suzanne, but it had better not happen again. That one was on the house, but the next one's going to cost you dearly; I promise you that."

"My father was a good man," I said, trying to calm my racing heart and my growing indignation. I hated the thought that this man had come into my shop, bought some of my goods, and then besmirched my late father's name almost as an afterthought on his way out the door.

"I never claimed that he was *all* bad," the man said as he crumpled up the top of the bag of donut holes again that he'd just bought from me. "But when Jack slipped, he slipped hard. How would your mother feel if everyone in town knew that he was a cold-blooded killer? Could either one of you stand continuing to live here with that kind of shame?"

"I keep telling you—you have the wrong man. My father's name was Thomas, and no one in his life ever called him Jack."

"Maybe not in your time, but ask your mother; she knows all about it."

That was another thing entirely. My mom was very good at keeping her own secrets; I knew that well enough, if her past history was any indication. "You come in here and tell me that my dad was a killer and you just expect me to trust you. If what you're saying is true, where's your proof?"

The stranger looked around the empty shop. "If I'd known that your donut shop was going to be deserted this time of day, I would have brought it with me, but I'm afraid that you'll have to wait until later to see it."

"Go get it right now," I said. "I can wait. The sooner we get this cleared up, the better. I still don't believe a word you've told me."

"You don't have to take *anything* on good faith. I'm willing to wager that you're going to *have* to believe what I'm going to show you. Meet me at the town clock at midnight," he said. "I'll have the evidence then. In the meantime, you are not to speak a word to the police about our little conversation, and that includes your boyfriend. Don't even think about telling your friend the mayor, either, and most especially, your mother is not to know that we spoke. If you tell *anyone* else about our conversation before I show you what I've got, it's not just your dad's *reputation* that will be at risk."

"Is that a threat?"

"Think of it as more of a promise."

"Sorry, but I can't make it at midnight," I said. "I don't get up until two in the morning, and I need every bit of sleep that I can get until then."

He looked surprised by my reaction. "Isn't it worth losing a few hours sleep to learn the truth about your dad?"

"Tell you what. I'll compromise. I'll meet you at the clock at one a.m."

"If that's the way you feel, let's just forget it. I'm taking the offer off the table. Remember, you had the chance to save your father's precious name, but you blew it."

Now I'd done it. I'd pushed the man too far. "Okay, midnight it is," I agreed before he could get out the door. "Should I bring some cash with me? That's your angle, isn't it? If you were hoping for a big score, I'm afraid you that you've badly misjudged your blackmail victim. Look around. Does Donut Hearts look like it's breaking even, let alone making enough to show a profit?"

"We both know that *you're* not the one in the family with money, Suzanne," he said.

"Mister, if you think that you have a better chance getting it from my mother, you're even crazier than I thought. She'll steamroll over you like you weren't even there."

"Once you see my evidence, I'm convinced that you will be able to persuade her to pay *whatever* I'm asking."

"I have serious doubts about that."

"They'll be gone at midnight," he said. "What I'm asking is quite reasonable, and worth every dime it's going to cost you."

He was gone in a flash, and I felt my hands shaking a little after I was alone again. Confrontation usually did that to me, and this guy had been more unpleasant that most. What did he believe that he had against my father, something that was so potentially disastrous to his memory that he thought my mother would actually pay to have it kept silent? I thought about calling Jake and getting his opinion despite the stranger's dire warnings, but my state police inspector boyfriend was wrapping up a case in Hickory, and I didn't want to disturb him. I could have called Grace Gauge, my best friend and number one ally in fighting crime in April Springs, but I decided to wait until I had more information before I called in my reserves.

In the meantime, I had to find a way to wait out the time until I heard what the stranger had to say about my sweet old dad.

The rest of the day was not going to be easy, I knew that for sure. The very thought of my dear, departed father raising his voice, let alone his hand, was beyond comprehension. I knew in my heart that it would all turn out to be an elaborate hoax, or a case of mistaken identity, but there was one small flicker of doubt in the back of my mind. Jake often said that none of us were beyond murder if the stakes were high enough, and though I wasn't sure *how* I felt about his philosophy, I couldn't bear to think of my father that way.

"Suzanne, do you have a second?" my ex-husband Max asked as he walked into the donut shop at ten forty-five.

"I have fifteen minutes before I close, Max. Do you need some donuts for your seniors theatre troupe?" Max was a part-time actor, mostly regional commercials and local theatre, not that he hadn't had his share of the national limelight. I'd been lucky enough, if anyone could ever call it that, to catch him with another woman just as his biggest national commercial hit the airwaves. My divorce settlement had paid for Donut Hearts free and clear, and it was a good thing that I owned the property, especially if I had to depend on slow periods like I was going through now in the summer heat.

"No, we're taking the summer off. Too many of my actors are in Boone, Asheville, and West Jefferson. When the temperatures rise, they flee en masse to the mountains."

"Then what brings you by?" I asked as I started cleaning off a few of the tables I hadn't had a chance to get to yet.

"As a matter of fact, I need your help," he said.

I dropped the plate in my hand, and I was glad that it was plastic as it bounced up from the floor.

"Come on. It's not that shocking," he said as he knelt down to retrieve it for me.

As Max handed the plate back to me, I replied, "You should see how it looks from my point of view." Our parting hadn't been the most amicable of splits, given the circumstances, but I was finally managing to put it behind me, mostly because Jake was in my life these days, and Max, on his very best of days, was nothing but a pale imitation of the man in my life now.

"Okay, I'm willing to admit that it sounds kind of screwy on the face of it, but I have nowhere else to turn," he explained. I looked into his eyes for a second, and saw that he was on the level about that. I hadn't learned much in my time married to the man, but I'd at least learned that much.

I put the plate in a plastic bin near the door, and then I led him to one of our sofas.

He took the chair across from me, and I asked him, "What exactly is going on?"

"It's about Emily," he said.

That's all that I needed to hear. As I started to get up, I said, "Max, you need to leave Emily Hargraves alone." Emily ran our local newsstand, Two Cows and a Moose, named after her childhood stuffed animals who still laid watch over her store from a high shelf by the register, adorned in whatever seasonal outfits Emily made for them.

"Suzanne, please don't turn your back on me. I think I've fallen for her," Max said.

I'd never heard him say anything quite like that since I'd known him. "How does Emily feel about you?"

"She won't even talk to me, thanks to you."

"Hang on a second," I said. "You're not actually blaming

this on me, are you?"

"No, of course not," Max replied. "Well, maybe just a little. If you hadn't told her all of those bad things about me, we'd still be together."

I shook my head, and then I asked him, "Max, was *anything* I told her a lie?"

"What?"

"Think about it carefully before you answer. Did I tell Emily a single thing about you that wasn't true?"

"No," he said after a moment or two, "at least not the old me. But I've changed, Suzanne. I've settled down quite a lot in the past year. A lot has happened to me."

I knew without asking what he was talking about. He'd lost a girlfriend, and then he'd been accused of murdering her. I understood from firsthand experience how an accusation like that, no matter how unfounded it might be, felt. "I hear what you're saying, but you're giving me way too much credit here. Emily Hargraves does not live or die by my recommendations. She's a grown woman perfectly capable of making up her own mind without any help from me."

"Could you at least *talk* to her for me?" he begged. If he hadn't been an actor, I never would have doubted the sincerity in his expression. Then again, maybe he was just playing me for the thousandth time. I'd fallen for his smooth ways far more than once in the past.

"I don't know, Max. I'm not even sure what I could say to her that might make her change her mind about you."

"I just want one date, one opportunity to convince her to go out with me again, but she won't even discuss it with me."

"And you don't think that's your answer right there?" I asked softly, trying to cushion the blow of what I was saying.

"Suzanne, haven't you ever wanted a second chance in your life?"

I was about to say no when I realized that was what Jake had given me, another chance to love someone with all my heart, regardless of the consequences. "We both know that I have."

"Then help me. If you don't want to do it for me, then at least do it for love."

It might have come from a part he'd once played, but it worked on me nonetheless. "What is it exactly that you want me to say to her?"

"Just tell her that I'm begging her for one last chance. She can pick the place, the time, and anything else she wants. It's all that I'm asking."

I nodded, and then I looked back into his eyes. "Max, have you *really* changed? It wasn't all that long ago that you were trying to take advantage of her, and she stopped you dead in your tracks. Are you sure that you're not doing this just because you want to prove to yourself that you can get her?"

"I considered the possibility," Max admitted, something that truly startled me. "But in the end, it all boils down to the fact that I love being with her. Her laugh does something to me inside, and I could live off one of her smiles for days. She makes me want to be a better man than I am, and I never want to disappoint her."

My lands, it appeared that my ex-husband was honestly smitten.

"Okay. I believe you. I'll talk to her," I said. Before he got a word in, though, I added, "But this is it. I'm not going to beg, plead, or get down on my knees for you. I'll ask her, and *whatever* she says, I'm out of it for good."

"That's all I can ask," he said. "Thanks so much, Suzanne." Max looked at the mostly still-stocked cases behind me, tray upon tray filled with iced and glazed treats. "How much for everything that's left?"

"What? Are you crazy? You don't have to do that."

"I want to," he said as he pulled out his wallet. "I'm holding a little workshop at the theatre for the folks who can't afford to head off somewhere, and those will make a nice treat. What do you say? Don't give me a discounted price, either. I want to pay full retail."

"Max, I already said that I'll talk to Emily for you. This

isn't necessary."

"That's what makes it so much fun to do," he said.

I thought about arguing with him, but my mother had taught me that when someone wants to buy what you're selling, never try to talk them out of it. Just give them what they want, extend your hand for payment, and then say, "Thank you."

"Emma, grab some boxes. We've officially sold out for the day," I said as I opened the kitchen door and found my assistant just finishing up another sink full of dishes. Emma had left me, gone to college, and found that it wasn't for her. She'd been overjoyed to have her place back at Donut Hearts, and I was thrilled to have her.

"Who's the big spender?" she asked as she rinsed off the last plate and put it into the drying rack.

"Max," I said as I collected a few boxes so I could get started.

"What does he want?" she asked me with a grin.

"I'm playing Cyrano for him," I said.

"Suzanne, please tell me that you're kidding," Emma said. "Do I even want to know who's going to be on the other end?"

Since she and Emily were close, I decided to keep that to myself. "Does it matter? We can both leave after we box these up and clean up a little."

"Then I'm with you."

"Hello, Max," Emma said as she walked out into the dining area. "I hear that love is in the air."

"I hope so," Max said. "Can I give you a hand?"

"No, Suzanne and I have a system."

The pair of us boxed the donuts, all eleven dozen of them, and I did a little quick math to come up with a total. I was tempted to knock off a few bucks before I quoted Max a price, but then I remembered Momma's words again.

Max paid gleefully, and even managed to carry them all in one load, though he couldn't see where he was walking.

"Give me some of those and I'll help you," I said as I held

the door for him.

"Don't worry about me. I can do it," he said.

"Sure, you can, but there's no need to." I grabbed four of the full boxes, loaded with filled donuts from apple spice to zesty lemon, and then I turned back to Emma. "Hang around. I'll be back in a minute."

"Take your time," Emma said. "I'll start sweeping the front."

The heat was oppressive, stealing my breath away with its intensity when I walked outside. I feared for my donuts, and I was glad when we finally made it to the parking lot. Once we were at Max's car and had the donuts safely stashed away with the air conditioner blasting away on high, he turned back to me and asked, "Emma seems happy, doesn't she?"

"She's so glad to be back in town working at Donut Hearts, I could probably get her to work for nothing, not that I ever would."

"College isn't for everyone, is it?"

"Well, she's still going to the community college, and I suspect she'll try going away again in a few years, but for now, I'm thrilled to have her with me."

It was clear that Max had more on his mind than Emma's wellbeing. Finally, he asked me, "When are you going to talk to Emily for me, Suzanne? You know how close she and Emma are, so if you let something slip to her too soon, I'll be doomed from the start."

I had to bite my lip to keep from being snippy. "As soon as I finish shutting down for the day, I'll walk over to Two Cows and a Moose," I said. "Until I speak with Emily, I won't say a word to Emma about it."

"That's perfect. Do me a favor, would you? Call me no matter what she says, okay?"

That sounded fair to me, so I agreed. "Don't get your hopes up, Max. After all, I can only do so much."

"It's too late, they are already sky high," Max said with his characteristic grin. "Talk to you soon."

I walked back to Donut Hearts, not sure exactly what I

was going to say to Emily. I'd state Max's case, and then I'd let her decide without trying to exert any undue influence on her. Now that Max was gone, I realized that it had happened again. Somehow, my ex-husband had reached out beyond the grave of our marriage, and he had somehow managed to pull me back in.

At least he'd managed to distract me, if only for a few moments, from the stranger who'd come in threatening my father's memory, and if nothing else, I owed him something for that.

Chapter 2

"Hi, Emily," I said as I walked into Two Cows and a Moose a little later that day. Her stuffed animals were on their usual perch sitting together on a shelf above the register, and I was amused to find them all dressed in old-fashioned swimsuits, as though they were ready for a dip in the 1800s. They each wore big, bold sunglasses, and Emily had even added little patches of white that looked as though they all had sunscreen on their snouts. "My, aren't they dressed nicely today. They're ready for the beach, aren't they?"

She laughed. "Cow and Spots were fine with their outfits, but Moose had a fit about wearing the swimsuit I made him. He always *has* had such a quiet dignity about him, and there are times when he resists my best efforts to dress him up like his pals."

I had to look twice at her to see if she was kidding, and I still couldn't tell. Emily and her three stuffed-animal friends had shared a bond while she'd been growing up that was unreal at times. I wasn't a hundred percent sure that she didn't believe in her heart that they were real and carried on actual conversations with her, but if it was crazy, it was a kind of insanity that I could get behind. Whenever I was around the four of them, three stuffed and one human, I tended to suspend all disbelief myself, and there were moments when I expected one of them to chime into the conversation at any second. "How's business?"

"It's going great," she said. "This is one of my busiest times of years. Have you seen my new line of paperback novels?"

Leave it to Emily. If she found something her customers wanted, she did her best to make sure that she could satisfy their needs with one-stop shopping. There were three new racks of paperbacks, and not just for bestsellers, either. As I scanned the titles, I found a preponderance of brightly covered mysteries that were all warm and inviting. Some showed images featuring food, while others exhibited cats, crafty items, front porches, and warm surroundings.

"There are a lot of new mysteries, I see," I said.

"My clientele just lap them up," she replied. "And why not? There's something cozy and comforting about these books. Besides the usual readers, I get folks who tell me about going to visit loved ones in the hospital, or worse, trying to get over the loss of folks they loved, and they always seem to turn to this particular kind of book. There's something so reassuring about the small towns these authors write about, despite the prevalence of murder." Emily looked around her store, and upon seeing that it was mostly deserted, she added softly, "Don't tell anybody, but I'm writing one myself in my spare time."

"I didn't know that you were a writer," I said. "That's awesome."

"Well, I'm not one yet, at least not published," she admitted. "But I just had to try my hand at it."

"How's it going so far?" I asked her.

Emily frowned a bit. "It's harder than it looks, I'll say that."

"Anything worth doing is worth the struggle, though, wouldn't you say?" It wasn't the most subtle segue in the world, but it was all that I could manage.

"Something tells me that we're not talking about books anymore," Emily said.

"We aren't," I replied. "The real reason that I'm here is because of Max."

My friend's smile quickly faded. "Now he's roped you into this, too, has he? The man has some kind of nerve, Suzanne. I can't believe you agreed to help him, especially since you were the one who warned me about him in the first place."

"I know; believe me, it sounds crazy to me even as I'm doing it. He wants another chance with you."

"So he keeps saying," she replied. Her expression softened for a moment as she asked, "Do you think he deserves it?"

"That's not really a fair question to ask me, is it? All I'm saying is what happened between us shouldn't affect the two of you."

"Suzanne, he *cheated* on you."

"You don't need to remind me. But I do believe people have the capacity to change, don't you?"

"I'm not sure," she said after a few moments of silence. "Even if it's true, I doubt that it happens all that often."

"You won't get any argument from me," I said. "You should do whatever *you* want, but I wanted to just put it out there." I started to go, and then I decided that full disclosure was the best policy here. After all, I didn't want to take a chance on ruining our friendship. "Emily, he bought out my donut shop's inventory today, but only after I agreed to speak with you for him. That wasn't a requirement, though. I think Max did it out of sheer jubilation, but I didn't want you to hear about it and think that he bribed me into talking to you. I have too much respect for you *and* our friendship to do that."

"Suzanne, I would never believe for one second that you could be bought," Emily said, and then she added a wicked little grin as she said, "Not for donuts, at any rate."

"Don't kid yourself, he bought eleven dozen," I said with a laugh, happy that all was well between us. "So, what do you think you're going to do?"

"Hang on. Let me consult with my life coach experts." She walked over to her stuffed animals and asked, "You heard what the lady said. What do you guys think?"

I half-expected one of them to answer.

I didn't hear a reply, but perhaps Emily had. "That settles it. I'll do it, but there's only one condition that I'm going to insist on."

"I'm sure he'll do *anything* you ask to get another chance," I said, hoping that my mission of mercy didn't end up hurting my friend.

"It's not something that I need from him," Emily said. "If you believe that it's possible that Max has changed, *you* have to have dinner with us, too."

I would have rather broken my foot than go out with them on their date. "Are you sure I wouldn't just get in the way?"

"I'm positive. Take it or leave it. It's the only way it's going to happen."

I could tell that she wasn't about to budge. "When do you want to do this?"

"I'm free tonight if you are," Emily said with a smile. "Given your schedule, I assume we need to make an early evening of it. What about five?"

"I'll ask," I said, knowing that Max would break any engagement he might already have for another chance with Emily. "Do you have any place in particular in mind?"

"I think the Boxcar Grill is perfect, don't you?"

"Wonderful," I said, wondering what my friend, Trish— the owner of the grill—would say about me going out on a three-way date with Emily and my ex-husband. "I'll call Max and see what he thinks."

As I started to dial his number, Emily put a hand on my shoulder. "You should know that I won't hold you responsible for anything that happens tonight."

"That's comforting to know," I said, hoping that she meant it.

As I expected, Max didn't even hesitate accepting Emily's conditions.

It looked as though I had more plans tonight than just meeting a blackmailer at midnight under the town clock.

It was hard to say at that point *which* event I was looking less forward to doing.

It was time to go home, but I didn't know how I was going to possibly explain the two situations I'd gotten myself into to my mother. Before I'd moved back in with her after leaving Max, it wouldn't have been that difficult to duck her until I'd attended Emily and Max's big date and dealt with the man who'd accused my late father of murder, but since we were both living under the same roof again—a charming little cottage on the edge of the town park—things weren't quite so easy. She could read me like an open book, so I knew that keeping anything from her would be nearly impossible.

When I saw that her car was missing from our driveway as I parked my Jeep in its usual spot, I nearly whooped out in delight.

Inside, perched on the stairway so I wouldn't be able to miss it, was a note.

Dear Suzanne,

I'll be gone most of the afternoon, and into the evening. Phillip and I have plans.

Love,

Momma

P.S. Don't forget to eat something healthy.

Was there ever a time when our parents stopped trying to parent us? If there was indeed a cut-off age, it was pretty clear that I hadn't reached it yet.

At least I didn't have to explain to her what I was going to be doing later.

I glanced at the clock on the mantel over the fireplace and saw that I had plenty of time for a nap. Instead of going upstairs, though, where it was hotter than it had any right to be at this time of day, I turned on the ceiling fan above the couch, added a box fan's breeze, and settled down on the couch for a quick nap.

I kept dreaming that drums were pounding in the background as I built a snow fort, and it took me a second to realize that reality was encroaching on my sleep. I sat up, glanced at the clock as I rubbed the sleep from my eyes, and realized that I'd overslept.

Then the knocking started again.

"Hang on. I'm coming," I called out as I made my way to the door.

It was Grace Gauge, my best friend, and frequent co-

conspirator. Grace, slim and blonde, was a perfect contrast to my brunette hair and ample curves, and we fit together as though our destinies had been planned from the very start.

"I knew you must have been asleep," she said as I let her in. "Let's go grab a bite, unless you have plans with Jake or your mother tonight."

"I don't, but I can't," I said as I shut the door behind her.

"Wow, that's quite a cryptic answer," she said. "Care to fill me in?"

"Only if you don't mind listening while I grab a quick shower," I said as I hurried upstairs to my own little en suite.

"Sadly, I've got nothing better to do, so lead the way," she said with a smile.

Grace jumped on my bed while I headed into the bathroom, and I left the door open so we could chat while I got ready.

I started to bring her up to date on my dinner plans with Emily and Max when she walked into the doorway. "Suzanne, have you completely lost your mind?"

"I know how it sounds, Grace, but what could I do? Max really cares about Emily, and if I can lend them a hand, why shouldn't I?"

"Jake has turned you into a hopeless romantic, hasn't he? Or are you just hopeless? Do you honestly believe that your ex could *ever* change?"

"It's really not up to me to say, is it?" I asked. "*Emily's* opinion is all that matters. Besides, how bad could it be? We're eating at the Boxcar, and I'm going to be there the entire time."

"I've got to see this for myself. I'm coming, too."

I was afraid of that. My friend's sense of curiosity might have been even bigger than mine. As I rinsed the shampoo out of my hair, I said, "Grace, it's sweet of you to offer, but I've got this covered."

"Did you honestly think that I was tagging along to *help*?" she asked with a laugh. "This has "train wreck" written all over it. I wouldn't miss it for the world."

I shut off the water and grabbed a towel. "I'm not about to try to keep you from going to the Boxcar, but I can't invite you to our table. You know that, don't you?"

"You don't have to worry about me. I'll be a discreet distance away. Do you think the next table over will be far enough?"

I had to laugh at that myself. "Just try not to be *too* obvious about it, okay?"

"I'll try, but you should know better than to ask me to make promises that I can't keep. So, what are you doing after the Great Debacle, I mean, the Big Date?"

"I'm planning on heading back here and going straight to bed," I said as I dried off and put on my robe.

"Why so early? You usually stay up at least until eight."

"As a matter of fact, I have a meeting at midnight," I replied. I wasn't going to let this stranger take over my life anymore and dictate what I could and could not do, though he'd done a pretty good job of it so far. The problem was that I didn't trust him, so why would I meet him in the middle of the night without telling anyone else what I was up to? If I told Grace about it, I at least knew that she'd insist on being there, lurking somewhere in the shadows and out of sight.

"Is Jake coming over from Hickory?" she asked.

"No, it's not with him. I'm meeting a blackmailer," I replied.

Grace glanced at me, and there was no doubt in my mind that she knew that I was being perfectly serious. "Talk," she said after positioning herself squarely back on my bed. "Hang on. What exactly have you done recently that you could be blackmailed for, and why am I just hearing about it now? Suzanne, if you're going to get into trouble, I'm disappointed that you didn't include me. It must have been fun if someone's trying to blackmail you for doing it."

"Are you quite finished?" I asked.

"Not yet. So, answer the question; why didn't you invite me?"

"To the meeting tonight?" I asked as I picked something

out of my closet that was a little nicer than my normal jeans and T-shirt.

"That, but more importantly, to whatever it was you were up to when you got caught."

"It's nothing that *I* did," I said. "It's about my father."

Grace's smile vanished quickly as she sat up on the bed. "Tell me everything."

I told her all I knew as I finished dressing, and by the time I was ready to head back downstairs again, she said, "That's it. I'm not taking no for an answer. I'm going with you tonight."

"You can't," I said. "What if he's watching the house? It would be too easy to spy on me here, and if he sees that I'm not leaving alone, he might not show up at all."

Grace nodded. "I can see your point, but there's no way that you're going alone. Tell you what. I'll get there half an hour early and hide in the shadows. I'll have my cell phone ready to call Chief Martin the second this guy does anything suspicious."

"I'd appreciate that," I said, "but you need to call the dispatcher. The chief is going to be out with Momma."

"Do they typically stay out until one in the morning?" Grace asked. "Good for her."

"I don't keep tabs on her coming and going," I said. "But then again, maybe that's because I don't want to know."

"I totally understand that," she said. "Wow, you are in for a busy night. No wonder you were taking a nap."

"Try working my hours and see if you can keep from it," I answered.

"No, thanks. I like my job just fine, thank you very much." She studied her outfit and asked, "Should I change, too?"

"Why should you? You look better in your casual clothes than I do all dressed up, and besides, you aren't going out on this date yourself, remember?"

"Oh, that's right. I forgot. What time is the big event, anyway?"

I glanced at the clock. "It's in ten minutes."

"My, aren't they the early bird diners," Grace said.

"I'm afraid that's in deference to me. Emily wanted me there to chaperone, and that was my one condition."

"Then by all means, let's go."

She walked out of the house with me, and as I locked the door behind us, she said, "I'll go ahead and meet you there. I don't want them to think that I'm there to spy on them."

"Wouldn't that be true, though?" I asked with a smile.

"Of course it is, but I don't have to be that obvious about it."

I waited for Grace to drive away in her company car, and then I got into my Jeep. The air conditioner had a tough time with the heat we were having, and by the time I got to the Boxcar Grill, I was still too warm for my own comfort. Thankfully Trish believed in air conditioning, the colder the better. I'd grabbed a sweater on the way out of the house, no matter how crazy it must have seemed to any onlookers if they'd been watching me, but I knew that I'd most likely need it for Trish's diner.

"Hey there," I said to her as I walked into the converted boxcar just across the park from Donut Hearts. I could have walked there just as easily, but that would have meant enduring more heat directly, something I was not all that eager to do. The cold hit me like a wave at the beach, and I quickly put my sweater on.

"Hey yourself. We thought you'd never get here," Trish said with a smile, her ponytail bobbing as she gestured to a table in the back.

I looked and saw that Max was sitting there waiting impatiently, dressed in his best suit, with a dozen red roses on the table in front of him.

"Has Emily shown up yet?" I asked.

"Three times, as a matter of fact. I'm supposed to call her when you get here, so give me a second and I will."

Before she dialed, I said, "Have you heard about what's going on?"

"That you're playing matchmaker with your ex-husband and one of your best friends? I might have heard bits and pieces of the plan," she said with a smile.

"When you put it that way, I'm beginning to doubt my sanity agreeing to do this in the first place," I said.

Trish hugged me, and said, "Honestly, I think it's sweet of you. Why shouldn't everybody find love?"

"How about you?" I asked. "Any prospects on the horizon?" Trish was notoriously unlucky at love, though I hoped that someday she'd find someone, since she wanted it so badly. She'd just lost someone that she might have grown to love, but he was murdered before they could really find out what the future might hold for them.

"No, I've decided to take myself off the market," she replied.

"Seriously? You can't just give up."

"Maybe you're right, but it seems like the smartest thing that I can do right now. We'll see how this works out between Emily and Max, but if they can make it, I might just let you try matchmaking for me."

"Hang on, I never said I was a…" I stopped when I saw her grin. "You joke, but I might just try, anyway."

"Knock yourself out," Trish said. "You can't do any worse for me than I've managed for myself."

The diner's owner finished her call, and I made my way to Max's table, stopping to wink at Grace as I did so. To her credit, she wasn't at the *closest* table, but she was still within hearing range of anything above a whisper. Grace winked back at me as I made my way to Max's table.

"For me?" I asked as I scooped up the roses and pretended to inhale them. "Max, you shouldn't have."

"I didn't," he said as he quickly took them from me. "They're for Emily."

"I know that, you idiot," I said with a grin as I sat down. "You really *are* nervous, aren't you?"

"There's a lot riding on this, Suzanne," he answered.

I shrugged. "I can honestly say that I've never seen you

like this, Max."

"I know, right? I'm a man who's learning to follow his heart."

"Well, all I can say is that it's about time," I answered as I nodded my approval of his change of attitude.

"Are these too much?" he asked as he placed the roses down again.

"It depends on the message that you're trying to send."

"I want her to know that I'm serious about this," he answered.

"Well, they should do that, if nothing else."

Emily came in, looking gorgeous as well, and I began to feel that I was underdressed, even given the attire of the other diners around us. She walked up to the table, and Max stood up, something he'd neglected to ever do for me, but I wasn't about to tease him about it. He presented the roses to Emily, who accepted them graciously.

"I don't know what to do with them," she said as she looked around the diner.

"I'll take care of them," I answered, and then I took them to Trish. "Do you have a vase we can borrow?"

"I'm way ahead of you," she answered as she pulled one out from behind the counter. "That's the problem with men; they don't think things through."

"Hey, it could have been worse. He could have gotten her a corsage."

"I remember the one I got at prom," she said. "It was sweet."

"You were eighteen, too. Thanks."

"Happy to help," she said.

I made my way back to the table, and when I got there, I found them sitting in stony silence.

"What did I miss?" I asked.

"We were waiting for you," Emily said.

That was not a good sign. Was it going to be up to *me* to make conversation? I was there as a chaperone, not a conversation facilitator. "It's really hot out, isn't it?" I asked lamely.

And that's when Max saved the date.

"How are the guys holding up back at the shop? Moose must be roasting," he said.

"He was until I got him a box fan. Now he doesn't even mind the swimsuit."

"They're all in bathing suits now? How do Cow and Spots feel about that?"

"Spots thinks they're pretty, and he's just about convinced Cow of it, too."

"He always was the stylish one, wasn't he?"

They were off now, discussing the moods and foibles of Emily's three stuffed animals, and though it might have seemed just a tad crazy to anyone listening in on the conversation, it all made perfect sense to me.

Once the meal was over, Max excused himself to pay the bill, and Emily leaned over to talk to me. "He really *has* changed, hasn't he?"

"I'm not giving my opinion one way or the other at this point," I answered. "Besides, what I think shouldn't matter. It's all up to you."

"Well, dinner went well, at any rate. We'll have to wait and see about the rest of it."

"That sounds prudent," I answered. I wasn't about to commit one way or the other, but I had to agree with Emily. I knew that Max was smooth, but there had always been a 'slick' component to him in the past, and that was nowhere to be seen tonight.

"Thank you for coming tonight," Emily said as she squeezed my hand. "You did me a huge favor."

"I was happy to do it." That was a big fat lie, but one I didn't mind telling.

Emily frowned at me, and then said, "Suzanne, stop worrying about how it sounds. I need to know what you really think about all of this."

"Sorry, but I'm not *about* to get involved." Well, that was what I *should* have said. Instead, I replied, "I think he legitimately cares for you, and if tonight's any indication, I've got a hunch that he really *has* changed."

So much for my vow of neutrality.

"Thank you so much," she said to me as Max returned.

"What are you thanking *her* for?" Max asked.

"It's nothing. Suzanne and I were just chatting."

"Uh oh. That can't be good for me," he said, the worry clear on his face.

"Don't be so sure about that," she said as she stood and took his hand.

I'd never seen Max's face light up like that the entire time we'd been married, and to be honest, it kind of bugged me a little at first, but I quickly let it go. I had someone in my life, a man who mattered to me deeply. If Max could find that experience with Emily, more power to them both.

After they were gone, Grace motioned for me to join her.

"Wow, that went surprisingly well, didn't it?" she asked me, sounding a little disappointed that there hadn't been a better show.

"Better than I ever imagined. I just hope that I did the right thing sticking my nose into their business."

"Hey, whatever happens, from the sound of it, you gave Emily every chance to make up her own mind," Grace said. "Do you feel like some pie? I noticed that you mostly just picked at your meal."

"Can you blame me? It was one of the oddest conversations I've ever been privy to, and that's saying something."

Trish came back to Grace's table. "Who would have believed it? They both looked happy when they left."

"We're all amazed," Grace said. "Care to join us for some pie?"

She looked around at the crowded diner, and then Trish said, "Why not?"

"We don't want to take you from anything," I said.

"It's hard to imagine what I *wouldn't* do for pie," she said as she walked back up front.

"Are you nervous about tonight?" Grace asked in a soft voice after Trish was gone.

"A little, but I'm feeling better about it since I told you. Knowing that you're going to be close by is huge for me."

"I still think I should be standing right beside you when you talk to this guy. You shouldn't be alone."

"I can handle him," I said, hoping that it was true. I saw Trish approach with a tray full of pie. "Remember, not a word to anyone, Grace."

"My lips are sealed," she said.

Trish lowered the tray as she explained, "I've got apple, cherry, and pumpkin. Take your pick."

"Pumpkin?" I asked. "In August?"

"Hey, what can I say? My pie maker was homesick for Thanksgiving. There are other choices, you know."

"No, I want that one," I said as I reached for the golden orange slice.

"I don't have to tell either one of you that cherry's my favorite," Grace said.

"I knew that, and I had a hunch that Suzanne wouldn't be able to resist the pumpkin. I wanted the apple slice all along."

We all laughed at that, and we shared a few minutes of joy as we ate and caught up on the most mundane things in each other's lives. It was one of those moments I cherished about living in a small town.

No problem ever seemed too big when I had my friends around me.

Too soon, though, we were finished with our dessert. I paid for the pie and Grace left an even bigger tip, all under Trish's protests.

Once we were outside, I was surprised to nearly run over someone on the steps who was decidedly alone.

If the chief of police was heading into the diner to eat by himself, where exactly was my dear sweet mother?

MOM'S APPLE PIE DONUTS

No, my mother never made these, but who can resist the name? I love baking apple pies, so once when I was looking for something warm and tasty to make on a cold and rainy afternoon, I searched for some apples to no avail. Why not an apple pie donut? Some of my best work has been using what I have on hand, and this was no exception. This recipe includes apple pie spice, which consists of cinnamon, nutmeg, and allspice, and applesauce. These donuts are the next best thing to fresh apple pie, and after they are out of the oven or your donut maker, try them with powdered sugar while they're still warm. We also like dipping them in apple butter, and if we're feeling particularly decadent, we add a touch of butter to each bite first. Very tasty!

INGREDIENTS

MIXED
1 egg, lightly beaten
1/2 cup applesauce, natural and unsweetened
1/4 cup whole milk (2% will do)
1/4 cup butter, softened

SIFTED
1 1/4 cups flour, unbleached all-purpose
1/3 cup brown sugar, dark
2 teaspoons apple pie spice (cinnamon, nutmeg, and allspice)
1 teaspoon baking powder
1/4 teaspoon baking soda
1/4 teaspoon salt

INSTRUCTIONS

If you're using your oven, preheat to 365 degrees F before you start mixing.
In a bowl, beat the egg lightly, then add the applesauce, milk,

and butter. In a separate bowl, sift together the flour, brown sugar, apple pie spice, baking powder, baking soda, and salt. Add the dry ingredients to the wet, mixing well until you have a smooth consistency.
Put the batter into your donut pans or into your donut baker and bake for eight to ten minutes in your oven, five to six minutes in your donut baker, or until they're richly brown.

Yield 10-12 small donuts

Chapter 3

"Did you forget someone?" I asked Chief Martin.

"No, not that I know of," he replied.

"Where's Momma?" I asked him a little more pointedly.

"Suzanne, I don't have a clue. I didn't realize that she was lost."

The police chief looked as perplexed as I felt. Had their plans changed, or had my mother lied to me about what she was up to this evening?

"Sorry, I must have gotten my dates mixed up," I said. "I just thought that you two were going out tonight."

"We were, but something came up at the last minute," he answered.

"For you, or for her?" Grace asked. I wanted to shush her, but it was too late.

"Her, if it matters. Suzanne, you're acting a little oddly this evening, if you don't mind my saying so."

"Why should I possibly mind that?" I asked. "Have a good dinner."

"Thanks," he answered uncertainly. It was clear that our exchange had left the man a little off-balance.

When I turned around to look at him a few paces later, he was still standing there staring at me in open puzzlement.

"What was *that* all about?" Grace asked.

I explained about the note that I'd gotten from my mother, and Grace giggled. "Do you think it's possible that Dorothy is stepping out on him with another man?"

I couldn't imagine it, not for a second. "There's no way. If she had another date, she would have just told him about it. My mother doesn't believe in playing games when it comes to affairs of the heart."

"Then what could it mean?"

"I wish I knew," I said as I glanced at my watch. "If she's at the house, I'll ask her about it, but if she's not, I'm going to get to bed a little early tonight, since I have to get up before I really want to for that meeting. You don't mind if I take off early, do you?"

"Don't worry about me; I'm a big girl. I can take care of myself. I'll see you later tonight near the clock."

"I hope I don't see *you* while you're hiding in the bushes watching my back," I said.

"You'll never even know that I'm there. I'm as quick and as quiet as a cat," she said.

"I'll take your word for it," I said with a smile as I got into the Jeep and drove home. I was curious about what my mother had been up to, and this time I was hoping that she was home so we could talk. I wanted to know what she was doing, and if she was there, I decided that I was going to tell her about my meeting later that night. The more I thought about it, the more I realized that she deserved to know what was going on. If there was one person in April Springs who had more at stake in all of this than me, it was Momma. My father had meant the world to her, and if there was someone out there trying to sully his name with a murder accusation, she had every right to know about it, no matter what the blackmailer wanted.

Unfortunately, Momma wasn't home when I got there.

I decided to call Jake and get his insight on what I was about to do, but his phone went straight to voice mail, meaning that he was too deep into his investigation to pull out of it for anything short of a national emergency.

Since there was no one I could talk to, I decided to do the most sensible thing I'd done all day.

I went to bed, but not before setting my alarm clock for an hour earlier than I usually got up.

I had somewhere to be tonight, and I couldn't afford to miss it.

I was awake a full hour before my alarm was set to go off. I got dressed, and peeked at Momma's door when I got downstairs. It was closed, but that didn't mean anything; it had been closed when I'd gotten in the night before.

I started to grab my jacket on the way out the door, and then I wondered why I should bother. The temperature was in the mid-seventies, and we were supposed to get another hundred-plus day by the time all was said and done.

At least Momma's car was parked snugly beside my Jeep, so *sometime* in the night she'd made it back home. I planned to talk to her about her whereabouts after work, but for now, I had a blackmailer to meet.

As I drove down the darkened street toward Donut Hearts, I saw that the lights were off at Grace's, and her car was still in the driveway. No doubt she'd decided to leave it where it was and she'd walked down the road to her vantage point. The clock was close enough for her to walk past my donut shop and a few other businesses without generating too much of a sweat.

I was thankful that she was somewhere in the shadows watching over me.

I got to the clock, parked my Jeep, and then I got out and walked toward one of the benches in front of it. A man was already sitting there, all alone. Even though his back was turned to me, I had no doubt that it was my blackmailer.

"Well, I'm here," I said from ten paces away. "Where's this supposed evidence about my father that you promised to show me?"

There was no response.

Was he toying with me, or had he fallen asleep waiting for me to show up?

"Hello!" I said loudly. "Wake up!"

If he was sleeping, he was about to get a rude awakening.

I grabbed his shoulder to shake him awake, and he slumped off the bench and slid down onto the sidewalk.

Someone had clearly decided to settle accounts with the man before I'd had the chance to deal with him myself.

I was leaning over the body checking for a pulse when a police siren whooped once at me, and I turned to see the chief of police, a look of clear concern on his face as he opened his car door and raced toward me.

"It's not what it looks like," I told Chief Martin as he ignored me and got down on one knee to check for the man's pulse.

"Be quiet, Suzanne," he ordered.

For once, I decided to listen to him.

That's when I remembered Grace. Why hadn't she come out when the chief showed up? "Grace? Are you there?" I called out into the darkness.

"Suzanne, I'm warning you," he said.

"I don't understand. Grace was supposed to meet me here," I said, stretching the truth just a little. "What if she's hurt?"

Chief Martin stood up from the body and pulled out his handgun. "Stay right here."

"With him?" I asked as I gestured to the corpse. "Forget it. I'm coming with you."

He started to argue the point, but then he must have realized how futile it would have been. "Fine. Just stay behind me, and don't do anything stupid. Do you understand?"

"I'll behave myself," I said, meaning every word of it.

"Now, where exactly was Grace supposed to be?"

I couldn't really answer that, not without giving away why I was there. "I'm honestly not sure."

"Then you don't even know for sure that she was ever here in the first place. Call her."

I took out my cell phone and hit the number three for speed dialing. Momma was one, Jake was two, and Grace was three.

After nearly eight rings, I was ready to give up when she finally answered.

"Suzanne, I'm so sorry. I must have fallen asleep! Are you all right?"

"Not by any definition of the word," I said. "He's dead."

"Who's dead? The blackmailer? Do you need help hiding the body? Are you at the clock? I can be there in two minutes."

"I'm with Chief Martin," I said. "Maybe you should just stay right where you are."

"I'm so sorry. I know that I blew it. I don't know what else I can say."

"Grace, don't worry about it. We're good. Now, go back to sleep," I answered, and then I disconnected the call.

"So she's at home, safe and sound?" the chief asked after he put his weapon back in its holster.

"It turns out that she never left the house," I said, the relief thick in my voice. If Grace had done as I'd asked and come down to the clock, there might be more than one body there right now.

"And why was she meeting you at this time of night here by the clock, instead of at the donut shop?"

I had a decision to make. I could try to weave some kind of story on the spot to cover my tracks, or I could tell the truth. It didn't take long for me to realize that there was no way I could tell as many lies as I needed to in order to get me out of this. "That man came by the donut shop this morning and called my dad a murderer to my face," I admitted. "He demanded that I pay him off for his silence, but I didn't believe him. When I asked him for proof, he promised me that he'd have it with him tonight."

The chief took that all in, and then he asked, "Did you find anything on him?"

"I didn't even have time to look," I admitted. "You showed up the split second *after* I discovered that he was dead. How did you know that a body would be here?"

"It was an anonymous tip," Chief Martin said. "I hate those things, but we have to follow up on every last one of them. This time it turned out to be on the money, though, didn't it?"

"I didn't kill him," I protested yet again.

"I know that, Suzanne."

Wow, that was a real change of pace coming from him, to accept my innocence so easily. "How do you know that?"

"The body's already starting to stiffen up. That means that unless you hung around after you killed him waiting for me to show up, or you came back to get something you missed the first time, you probably didn't kill him."

"Thanks, Chief. That's such a relief hearing you say that."

"Don't go thanking me just yet. I still need to hear everything you know about this guy." It was clear by his expression when the next thought struck him. "Did you tell your mother about this man?"

"No. I never breathed a word about it to anyone but Grace."

He frowned. "I don't mean to sound rude, Suzanne, but that's not like you, is it? I have a hard time believing that you didn't even tell Jake."

"I tried, but my call went straight to voice mail," I answered.

An ambulance parked on the street by the clock, and paramedics got out to examine the body. It didn't take them long to realize that he was a lost cause. "There's nothing we can do, Chief," one of them said. "Want us to bag him up for you?"

"Not until my guys get here. Thanks for coming so fast."

"All part of the service. Call us if you need us."

Before they were gone, two of Chief Martin's deputies showed up, including one who was a frequenter of my donut shop. Officer Grant nodded to me as he approached, but he didn't say a word. Our friendship had gotten him into hot water on more than one occasion, and I didn't consider it a slight in the least that he came as close as he could to ignoring me.

Grant had a large, thick bag with him, and Chief Martin said, "Get pictures and video of *everything*."

"Got it, Chief," he said, and then Officer Grant got to work.

To the other officer, Chief Martin said, "Take your flashlight and start a perimeter search of the area."

"What exactly am I looking for?" the officer asked.

"In general, anything that looks suspicious, or doesn't belong here. Specifically, we're looking for the murder weapon."

"How was he killed?" the officer asked. I thought it was a reasonable question, but the chief just frowned. "We haven't determined that yet. Just keep your eyes open."

"Will do," the man said as he turned on his thick police flashlight and started his search.

"Should I go home?" I asked the chief as his men went to work.

"Don't you have a donut shop to open?" he asked me.

"Sure, but I wasn't sure that you'd want me to open the place this morning after what happened here," I admitted.

"You might as well go ahead and work. I know where to find you if I need you."

"Good enough," I said as I walked down to Donut Hearts, leaving my Jeep parked right where it was.

Fifteen minutes later, I had fresh coffee, so I put some in cups for the crew, locked up the shop, and walked down to deliver the brews.

The chief took one gratefully, as did two of his other officers. Grant was busy at the moment, but I set one aside for him.

"Any luck so far?" I asked. "I still don't even know what killed him."

"From my preliminary examination, it appears that it was a blow to the back of the head," the police chief said. I was startled by how willing he was to share the information, but I wasn't about to point it out to him.

"Who would do something like that?" I asked, more out of curiosity than anything else.

"Off the top of my head, I can think of a couple of people who had a motive to want to stop him," the chief admitted.

"And I'm about to go wake one of them up and question her. Would you care to come along and soften your mother up for me?"

I knew the answer to that question without even having to think about it. "Sorry, but I've got donuts to make."

"Sure, I just bet you do," he said. "Thanks for the coffee."

"You're most welcome. And, Chief?"

"Yes?"

"Good luck with Momma. I have a hunch you're going to need it."

"I'm afraid that you're right."

I tried to linger at the crime scene, but the chief wouldn't leave until I was safely locked back in my donut shop. I didn't have much choice, so I got started with the morning's cake donuts. The entire time I worked, I kept wondering where Momma had been the night before, and just how long she'd been in bed when I woke up. I sincerely hoped that she didn't need me for an alibi. It wasn't that I wouldn't lie for her; if it meant saving her, I had no compunction about that, but I had a hunch she wouldn't let me perjure myself.

Police cars with their flashing lights were still filling the night when Emma walked into the shop. "What's going on out there?"

"There was a murder right beside the clock," I said.

My assistant barely hesitated a second before she asked, "Can I call Dad?"

Emma's father owned and ran the town's newspaper, and he paid for every tip he received, whether it was from his daughter or not. Why shouldn't Emma get a little extra cash from this mess? "Go ahead, but I don't have any of the details."

"That's okay, he'll get them on his own," she said, and then she hurriedly called him.

I was afraid that he'd do just as Emma had suggested, and that my family, and our good name, was about to get another bit of bad press. I just hoped that he *never* found out everything there was to know about the ties the murder victim had to the Harts.

Emma and I kept making donuts as the morning wore on, although I couldn't help but stare at the clock every thirty seconds as we worked. Why hadn't Momma called me yet? Was the chief still grilling her about the murder, despite their relationship? Would he have to bring someone else in to work on the case? I had mixed feelings about the prospect of Jake coming to town to investigate my family again. It hadn't been all that good an experience the last time that he'd done it, and I had *no* desire for it to happen again.

The phone finally rang, and I picked it up quickly, despite the dough still stuck to my hands.

"Momma?" I asked. "Are you okay?" As much as I'd wanted to, I couldn't keep the concern I was feeling for her out of my voice.

"It's all right, Suzanne," my mother said in that soothing tone she used when she knew that I was troubled by something. "Phillip just left."

"What happened? Did you know that this guy was in town? Did he talk to you about Daddy, too?"

Momma hesitated a moment, and then she confessed, "That's where I was yesterday evening. Apparently after he spoke with you at the donut shop, he decided that he'd be better off going straight to the source."

"It's not true, is it, what he said about Daddy?"

"Suzanne, we need to have a conversation about this, but I don't want to do it over the telephone."

I felt my heart stop. "Are you telling me that he really *did* it?"

"I don't know," she answered flatly. The words must have been as hard for her to say as they were for me to hear.

"Momma, how could you not know?"

"Suzanne, I'll be there in four minutes. We can discuss it when I arrive."

My mother hung up, and as I put my phone on the counter

so I could wash my hands, Emma said, "It might just be me, but that did not sound good."

I looked sternly at my assistant as I said, "You didn't hear anything just now, Emma, so there's nothing you need to share with your father, is there?"

Emma looked upset by my question, but it needed to be voiced nonetheless. "Suzanne, I would *never* betray your confidence."

"I appreciate that," I said, hoping that my gut instinct that she was telling the truth was on the money. "I just thought that it might bear repeating under the circumstances."

"Believe me, I get it," she replied, though it was obvious she had been a little hurt by my statement.

So be it.

I had a family to protect, and if some bruised feelings were the worst things that I caused, I would consider it a success. I looked at our progress in the donut-making process, and I saw that I could leave the yeast dough in Emma's hands when Momma showed up. "Can you handle cutting out the donuts and bismarks with the wheels by yourself while I talk to my mother when she gets here?"

"Of course," she said. "I can do it, but I won't be nearly as fast as we are when we work together. Should I call my mother in to lend us a hand this morning?" Emma's mother had stepped up and helped on the rare occasions I was away from Donut Hearts, and she'd said a dozen times over the years that she was available if we ever needed her again.

"No, that shouldn't be necessary. I just need you to stay here and work while I have this chat up front. If you need anything, improvise until I come back into the kitchen. Do we understand each other?"

"Yes, ma'am," she said.

"Thanks," I answered, softening my stance a little and easing my voice.

"I'm glad to do it. No matter what happens, I don't believe for a second that you or your mother are murderers," Emma said.

"I appreciate that, but I really don't want to talk about it. Do you understand?"

"Absolutely."

I went up front to wait on Momma, and I saw her drive up.

Before she got out of the car, I met her at the door. "Let's chat outside at the table." The temperature was beginning to get uncomfortable, even though the sun wasn't up yet, but it wasn't unbearable, and we needed our privacy for this particular conversation.

"That sounds prudent to me," she said as she took a seat. "I don't suppose you have any coffee, do you?"

"I'll be right back." Inside, I grabbed two mugs, filled them up, and then rejoined my mother outside.

My mother took a long sip, sighed, and then she said, "That is delightful."

"I'm glad you like it. Now talk, Momma, and don't leave anything out."

She nodded. "I suppose we should have had this conversation years ago, but there never seemed to be a good time to do it."

"Right about now seems like the perfect opportunity to me," I said.

"Very well." It was clear that Momma was still reluctant to begin, but after a few moments, she sighed once, and then she began to explain. "After your father and I were married just over seven years, we separated."

"What?" I asked incredulously, nearly coming out of my chair in reaction to her statement.

"Suzanne, this will all go a great deal smoother if you keep your comments to yourself until I get through this. There's a *reason* that there's a cliché surrounding the seven-year itch in marriage, and I'm afraid that your father had it. At the time, he was dissatisfied with his life in general, including me, and so he moved out of April Springs to an apartment in Union Square, and it was seven months before he came home, begging me for my forgiveness."

"And you must have given it," I said, forgetting her request that I keep silent, "since you two ended up together again."

"Oh, it was difficult enough swallowing my pride, but I finally found a way to do it. I loved your father, and in a way, I understood his motivations. But before I would let him come back home, I told him that I could forgive his behavior once, but that if he ever tried to leave again, we were through forever. I wouldn't recommend ultimatums for most couples, but it worked for us. For the sake of our marriage's fragile state, we decided not to discuss what we'd done during our separation. In all the years afterwards, he never offered me a single clue about his time without me, and I never asked for any details. We were together, and that was ultimately all that mattered."

I tried to imagine letting Max off the hook for taking off on me for almost a year, but I couldn't fathom the circumstances where I'd even begin to consider it. Evidently my mother had a much more forgiving heart than I had.

Either that, or she had loved her husband a great deal more than I'd loved mine.

"Suzanne, I hope you don't think less of me because of this," Momma said as she stared down at her coffee mug. "I know that it wasn't the strongest thing I could have done given the circumstances, but I didn't know what else to do."

I leaned forward as I hugged her. "You're kidding, right? To be honest with you, I think that it's the strongest thing I've ever heard of anyone doing."

"I don't see how," she said, clearly a little confused by my response.

"Momma, if you could swallow your pride and let Daddy back into your life after he abandoned you like that, it just shows me how strong you were. I can tell you one thing; it's more than I'd ever be able to do."

"I worried that it would look like weakness in your eyes."

"I don't see it that way. You weighed what you'd lose if you turned him away, and then you made a deal that you could live with. Let me ask you something. If he'd left again, how would you have reacted?"

"I'd have had his things removed from the cottage before he hit the end of the street," she answered without hesitation.

"And were you two happy after he came back?"

"Gloriously," she admitted. "It doesn't hurt to mention that ten months after he came home, you were born. We grew more and more in love with each passing year until the moment he passed away."

"Then it was the right decision," I said. "Now, enough about the past. Let's talk about the present. Tell me all about what happened yesterday."

"Well, as you know, I had a date with Phillip, but when Mr. Briar called me, I canceled our plans. Suzanne, when I wrote you that note, I wasn't lying. I planned on being out on a date, but that telephone call changed everything."

"Was that his name? I never heard it myself."

"I told him that I wouldn't talk to an anonymous stranger, so he supplied that as his name, whether it was true or not."

"Did he ask you to meet him at the clock, too?" I asked.

"No, we found a discreet spot in the park under the bonsai plum tree." There was a particular tree that we both loved in the park that had suffered some severe storm damage during an ice storm a few years before. Instead of cutting it down, as any sensible arborist probably should have done, ours tried to save it, trimming the limbs and shaping the remainder of the tree into the world's largest bonsai sample. The nearby bench offered a nice screen from most places in the park, and more than a few teenagers had found it a good place to get a little better acquainted since.

"Did he tell you what this blackmail attempt was all about?"

She nodded as she took another sip of her coffee. "It appears that while Thomas was living in Union Square, Mr. Briar's brother, Blake, was struck and killed while crossing the street."

"What does that have to do with Dad?"

"Evidently, Thomas's car was stolen the day before, and though there was enough evidence at the time for the police to exonerate him, Morgan Briar was never convinced of your father's innocence."

"It's not all that uncommon for folks in hit-and-runs to report their cars stolen, is it?" I asked, my heart sinking a little.

"Suzanne, your father would never do something so cowardly," she said sternly.

"He ran out on *you*, didn't he?" I asked, suddenly resenting the man that I had adored growing up.

"Listen to me, young lady!" my mother snapped at me. "I will not allow you to judge your father for what he may have done in his weakest moment. His integrity was *never* in doubt. Besides, you don't know the whole story about our split, and if I have anything to say about it, you never will. Do we understand each other?"

"Loud and clear," I said. It was odd, but I'd always thought of my parents as just that, two people who had raised me together, and mostly that was the end of it. The idea that they'd had lives before I was born just never entered my stream of consciousness. Boy, was I going to have to adjust my thinking as far as that was concerned. "I'm curious, Momma. What evidence did Mr. Briar offer you to back up his assertion of Daddy's culpability in his brother's death?"

"All he had with him were a faded police report, an old letter, and a newspaper account of the tragedy. As far as I was concerned, it wasn't *proof* of anything."

"Did he honestly expect you to pay him to keep that quiet?"

Momma frowned, and then she explained, "Actually, the letter was the linchpin to his blackmail scheme.

It was from your father to Blake Briar, and in it, he threatened to kill the man."

Chapter 4

"He did *what*?" I asked.

"The letter explained that they had started a new business together, and Blake cleaned out their joint account without warning your father what he was doing. Thomas threatened legal action, and if that didn't work, your father said that the retribution would be worse than Blake could imagine. There was definitely more than a hint of a threat in the tone of that letter. Thomas said at one point that he'd wring Blake's neck if he didn't get his money back."

"Surely Morgan showed the police that letter," I said.

"He said that he did, but he claimed that the chief was one of your father's cronies, so the police refused to take it seriously. I told him that the entire premise was preposterous, but Morgan claimed to have an ace in the hole that he wasn't going to tell anyone about, real proof about your father's culpability."

"What did you do?"

"I slapped his face," Momma said, "but I never killed the man." She looked at me oddly, and then she asked me, "Suzanne, why are you smiling?"

"Truth be told, he was probably getting tired of being slapped by the time you hit him. I took a swing at him myself earlier in the day, and I made pretty good contact."

"Like mother, like daughter, I suppose," she said with a subtle smile.

"And I'm more proud of it than I could ever say," I answered. "What happened after that?"

"I stormed off as he yelled threats in my direction that I'd be sorry, but I didn't even hesitate to go. The man evidently seriously misjudged the women he was trying to blackmail. I have to wonder if we were his only victims, though."

"Why do you say that?"

"He wasn't nervous at all when he asked me for one

hundred thousand dollars," my mother said. "It was as though he'd practiced the request a dozen times before he made it of me, and I have to wonder if the man made it a habit of extorting money from other people. Perhaps one of his other victims caught up with him, and we had the misfortune to have it happen in April Springs while he was pursuing us."

"One way or the other, I need to dig into this," I said as I finished my coffee. "We can't just leave it up to the police."

"I agree. Suzanne, I believe an investigation is in order outside of official channels this time," she said. My mother hadn't been all that thrilled with my past snooping, but this was a matter of not just family honor, but our freedom and reputations as well. "Though I admit that I would feel better if Jake were involved unofficially."

"I keep calling him, but my calls go straight to voice mail. If I don't hear from him by noon today, I'm driving to Hickory to speak to him face to face." I reached out and patted her hand. "Don't worry, Momma. We'll figure out who killed Morgan Briar."

"I have no doubt that you will," she said as she stood up. Before she left, Momma said gently, "Suzanne, I know that you confide in Emma quite a bit, but it might be prudent to keep her out of the loop this time."

"I'm way ahead of you," I said. "Why do you think we stayed out here instead of inside where it's air conditioned?"

"I'm glad that we're in agreement, then. We'll discuss this later, but in the meantime, you have donuts to make, don't you?"

"Yes, it seems as though there are *always* donuts to be made," I said as I hugged her one last time. "Good bye, Momma, and thank you."

"For what? Dredging up the past with painful memories? I'm not entirely sure that you should be thanking me for doing that at all."

"I'm thanking you for trusting me enough to share your history with my father, warts and all," I replied.

After I walked back into the kitchen, Emma smiled brightly and showed me what she'd done in my absence. We didn't say a word about my conversation with Momma, and for a couple of hours, everything felt right with the world again.

"Hey, Chief, how are things going so far?"

"I'm guessing that you've already talked to your mother," he said, hanging his head a little low. I'd been waiting on customers all morning, and everyone was speculating about the mystery man who'd been murdered, though no one had tied him to me or my family yet. I knew that was just a matter of time, though.

"As a matter of fact, she came by the shop right after you left our place," I answered.

Chief Martin ran a hand through his hair. "I've got to tell you, I'm not exactly sure what I should do with this mess. Have you talked to Jake lately?"

"No, not in the past few days. Why?"

The police chief nodded. "I can't get him on the phone either, and truth be told, I could use his advice."

I thought about tweaking the law officer a little, but I realized how much it must have cost him to come ask me for help in finding my boyfriend. "If it's any consolation, I can't get him to answer my telephone calls, either. When he's hip-deep in a case, it takes a real emergency to get his attention."

"At least I know now that he's not just ducking me, so that's good news." The chief looked at my display cases, and I saw his gaze linger over the chocolate iced éclairs.

"Would you like one? It's on the house."

He was clearly tempted, but after a few seconds of struggling with his inner demons, the police chief shook his head. "I'd better not. I've got seven more pounds to lose before I'm back to my weight in high school."

"How much have you lost altogether?" I asked, sincerely curious about his weight loss. It had all begun the day he'd started courting my mother, and the man must have gone through at least three pants sizes since.

"Not enough," he replied. "If you talk to Jake, ask him to give me a call, would you?"

"I'll try, but can't make any promises about when that might be."

He nodded. "I understand. Well, I've got to run."

Half an hour after the police chief left, I was thinking about shutting down early for the day when the front door opened, and I nearly propelled myself across the counter when I realized that it was Jake.

After giving him a big hug and a matching kiss, I asked, "What's the idea, ducking my phone calls, Mister?"

"You know that I'd never do that unless it was important, but I was about to nab a bad guy, so I didn't really have time to call you back."

I leaned back as I asked, "Did you at least catch him?"

"As a matter of fact, he's sitting in a jail cell right now, though who knows how long he'll stay there. The man has more attorneys at his disposal than we do."

"What did he do?" I asked. Jake didn't like to discuss his cases while they were active, but he usually didn't mind after he'd made an arrest.

"There are some things that I'd rather not talk about right now, if it's all the same to you. Has there been anything exciting happening around here since we last spoke?"

"Well, let's see. Oh, yes. There was a murder early this morning at the town clock, and Momma and I are both involved it up to our eyebrows."

For a second Jake clearly thought that I was joking, but then he saw my intent expression. The joy of making an arrest earlier left him, replaced now by an expression of worry. "Tell me all about it."

After I brought him up to date, he said, "Suzanne, this is too big for you to handle on your own. This case spans decades."

"I've got a hunch the chief of police feels the same way

about it himself. He asked me to have you call him the second I saw you."

Jake shook his head. "There's another call that I need to make first."

"What could be more important than this?" I asked.

"I've got a hunch that I'd better make a preemptive phone call before my boss gets the same idea about who should be handling this case."

"Are you saying that you're not willing to help me out?" I asked, more than a little disappointed that Jake would duck this.

"There's a great deal more to it than that. Suzanne, you know that I'll give you all of the help I can. It's the April Springs police I'm planning to turn down." Jake frowned, furrowed his brows, and then asked me, "How would you feel if I took a week off and helped you dig into this case on my own?"

"Do you think you can really swing it? You know that I'd love it."

He smiled as he reached for his cellphone. "There's only one way to find out. I'll be right back."

As Jake stepped outside to make the call to his boss, I started getting ready to close the shop for the day. We didn't have that many treats left, mostly because Emma and I had made smaller batches of all of our donuts and other goodies earlier. That had gotten to be our habit recently after the decline in sales we'd been experiencing. We both hated throwing treats away, but the church had just about stopped taking our donations. It wasn't the best way to handle the slump, but I couldn't exactly go out, pull customers in off the street, and *make* them eat our donuts.

Jake came in a few minutes later with a frown on his face.

"No luck?" I asked. "That's okay. I understand. At least you tried."

"It's not over yet," he said. "I told my boss that he could give me the week of vacation I've got coming to me, or he'll just have to find another investigator to take my place."

"Jake, we've been over this before. You can't jeopardize your job making threats like that."

"I'm not," he said. "I happen to know that he got a memo instructing him to urge all employees to take their vacations this year so the state won't be in a position where they have to pay the accrued days off in cash at the end of the year. He just needed a nudge, that's all. Besides, the only thing I have on my schedule for the next few weeks is babysitting the governor. If he needs *that* done, he can do it himself."

Ten seconds later, Jake's phone rang. This time he stayed close by. "Yes, sir. Very good, sir. I'll check in with you next week. Thank you, sir."

"What do you know? I got it," Jake said with a smile as he hung up.

"There were no more waves at all?"

"In the end, there really wasn't much that he could do about it. He kind of surprised me, though. He's going to do as I suggested and take the protection detail himself. So, are you about finished here? We need to get started digging into this case."

"You're a real go-getter today, aren't you?"

"Suzanne, the way I see it, the quicker we solve this, the more time we get to spend together *not* focusing on murder."

"That sounds like a great plan to me," I agreed as I started cleaning the shop at a quicker pace. Frankly, I *loved* the idea of having Jake focus his skills entirely on my investigation. It would be so nice having him on my side, and not working for law enforcement in any official capacity. I knew that Grace wouldn't mind Jake's help, since she'd suggested it a few times herself in the past. I just hoped that we could all work together as well as Grace and I normally did, but only time would tell.

"I just had a thought," I said on the spur of the moment. "If we solve this case early, I'll turn the donut shop over to Emma and her mother for a few days, and we can take a real vacation together. How does that sound?"

"It's the best incentive that I've ever had to solve a case," he replied with a grin.

"So, where should we start?"

Jake thought about it, and then he said, "First of all, I need to do a little investigative work to see where things stand."

"That sounds great," I said. "Who should we talk to first?"

"Suzanne, I'm not at all certain that my sources will be forthcoming if you're with me. Some of the officers I need to speak with may be a little reticent to share what they know around a civilian."

"Let me get this straight," I said, being sure to keep my voice calm and level as I spoke. "The first thing you're going to do on our joint investigation is leave me behind, is that right? I'm not sure that I like the way this is headed."

My boyfriend took my hands in his as he said, "Suzanne, you've told me on more than one occasion that folks around here will tell you things that they won't tell law enforcement. Well, that cuts both ways. A great many cops will tell me things that they would never dream of sharing with you."

"So then we're going our separate ways after all?" I didn't like the sound of that at all.

"Don't look at it that way. We're both trying to solve a murder. We'll compare notes at the end of every day, and if there's something I can bring you in on my end of it, I promise you that I'll do it."

I thought about what Jake had just said, and though it made sense on one level, I hated the idea of being shut out of my own investigation. Still, what choice did I have?

"Okay. You work the proper police angles, and Grace and I will snoop on our own."

"Have you even asked her to help you yet?" Jake asked.

"No, but I doubt that she'll protest the idea. Grace's hours are pretty flexible, and she hasn't turned me down yet. Knowing that my father is involved, I'd be amazed if she didn't drop everything to lend a hand with the investigation. She was a big fan of my dad's, and the feeling was mutual. Grace wouldn't like to see my dad's reputation tarnished in any way, and I know that she wouldn't want to see Momma accused of murder. She'll help."

Jake nodded, and then he asked me, "Will you check in with me every hour so we aren't working at cross purposes?"

His look of sincerity was so cute that it was almost hard to tell him the truth. "Of course not," I answered with a grin. "When Grace and I are investigating a case, we almost *never* seem to know where our leads end up, and we have to follow them wherever they go."

"All that I'm asking is that you keep me informed," he said a little sullenly. "It's not like you have to ask me for permission or anything before you do something."

A full and throaty laugh escaped my lips before I could stop it.

"What's so funny?" Jake asked me.

"I find it amusing that particular thought would even enter your mind." I kissed his cheek, and then I said, "Go do your digging, and Grace and I will start with ours. I promise that I'll call you if we find anything significant, and I'd appreciate it if you'd do the same. We can meet back up at the cottage for dinner tonight and discuss what we've been up to. Does that sound good to you?"

"It does. Are you sure you don't mind if we handle things this way?"

"Jake, whatever clears my mother of suspicion and saves my father's reputation is a-okay with me."

He didn't return my smile. Instead, after a full ten seconds, he asked, "Suzanne, there's something else that we need to discuss."

"I'm listening," I said.

With great reluctance, he asked me, "What if I discover that what Morgan Briar claimed was true in the course of my investigation? Do you really *want* to know what happened?"

"I do," I said without a moment's hesitation. "I'm not saying that it's not going to be painful to hear, but I have to know the truth about my father, Jake. I'm a grown woman; I can take it."

"And your mother as well?"

"She can handle it, too."

"That's not what I meant," Jake said.

"I know that, but I'm pretending to believe that it was. There's no doubt in my mind that my mother loved my father, but there's no way she would kill to protect his memory."

"I hope you're right," Jake answered solemnly.

"You can count on it." Things were strained between us at the moment, and I hated the feeling. I kissed him soundly, and then added, "Now go do some unofficial police work. And Jake?"

"Yes?"

"Thanks for helping. It means a lot to me."

"There's nothing else I'd rather be doing in the world," he said, and then he headed for his car.

As he did, I grabbed my telephone and called Grace.

She answered on the first ring. "That's spooky, Suzanne. I was just about to call you," she said.

"I've told you before, we have some kind of eerie psychic bond. Are you free right now?"

"For you? Absolutely," Grace said. That was one of the things I loved about her; she was always ready to throw herself into my cases.

"How would you feel about doing a little investigating with me? Is there room in your schedule by any chance?"

"After I fell asleep on you this morning and left you holding the bag alone? You'd better believe that I can make time for you," she said. "I just got back in, so I'll do *whatever* you ask me to. I *still* can't believe that I wasn't there for you when you needed me."

"Grace, stop apologizing, okay? If it had been me, I would have probably fallen asleep myself. We're good."

"No way. You wouldn't have dozed off like I did, no matter how much you protest otherwise. Where should we start?"

"I was thinking that a drive to Union Square might be in

order. We need to find out all we can about the Briar brothers, and we've got the best resource there is in town to tap into."

"We're going to go see the DeAngelis ladies, aren't we?"

"I can't think of a better place to start, and while we're there, maybe we can get a bite to eat, too."

"You don't have to sell me on Napoli's," she said. "I'll pick you up in three minutes."

"You'd better make it ten," I said as I glanced at my watch. I had to help Emma finish closing up for the day.

"Ten it is. See you soon."

I'd have to tell her about Jake joining our team on the way to Union Square, but at the moment, I had cleaning to do.

The only problem was that someone else had her own agenda.

I looked down the street, and Gabby Williams was walking toward me with a stride that told me that she wasn't approaching me for a social visit.

"Suzanne, do you have any fans?"

"I'd like to think that some folks love my donuts enough to call themselves fans," I said. "I'm sure that you have admirers yourself, Gabby." She ran a gently used clothing store called ReNEWed, and her business was the closest to my donut shop. That made us de facto neighbors, but it didn't mean that I still didn't have to watch my step around her. Gabby had the fastest, and the sharpest, tongue in all of April Springs, and it was *never* a good idea to cross her.

"Not that kind of fan, you nit," she said with a hint of aggravation in her voice. "My air conditioning went out at the shop and I'm roasting."

That was serious indeed. With the heat wave we were experiencing, there was no way a customer would stay in an unairconditioned spot any longer than they had to. "Have you called someone about it?"

"Yes, for all the good that it will do me. Since Tim died, I've had a devil of a time finding a decent repairman."

I knew too well what she meant. Tim had met an untimely fate near my cottage, and every time I walked past the Patriot's Tree, I glanced up at it with trepidation, remembering seeing his body swaying in the breeze. "Come on in. I think I have a few box fans stored in back, and you're welcome to use them as long as you'd like."

"I appreciate that," she said as she followed me into Donut Hearts.

Emma was just finished cleaning up the display cases, and she was about to say something when she saw that Gabby was with me. "Good morning, Gabby," she said. "May I get you something? Coffee, perhaps?"

"It's a thousand degrees in my store. Coffee is the last thing I need right now, young lady," Gabby replied.

"How about some ice water, then?" I asked.

"That would be more appropriate," Gabby said. "Emma can get the water for me while you're retrieving those fans."

I winked at my assistant as I headed for the back and found the fans in short order. As I carried them back to the front, I heard Emma say, "I belong right here, at least for now."

Leave it to Gabby to poke and prod, no matter how little time she had for being nosy.

"Here you go," I said as I grabbed a clean rag. "Let me just dust these off for you."

"I can do it myself," Gabby said as she reached for the fans. "Why exactly do you have these on hand?"

"Don't you remember my last summer experiment?" I knew that she did, since her complaints had been the main reason I'd stopped. The year before, in a summer that was much milder than the one we were going through at the moment, I'd propped the fans near the counter and opened the front door, hoping that the smell of donuts would be enough to draw customers inside. I didn't know if it would have worked one way or the other, because Gabby had insisted that I was contributing to the growing air pollution that only she seemed to be able to sense.

"Ah yes, how could I forget when all of April Springs smelled as though a donut factory had just blown up."

I decided to take the high road and let that one go, mainly because Grace would be on her way soon, and I had work to do before she arrived. "Here you go. I hope they help."

Gabby seemed to take my capitulation with more curiosity than grace, but in a moment, she was gone, along with the box fans, and I got back to business.

As Emma and I cleaned, I asked, "It didn't take her long to take a jab at you, did it?"

Emma just grinned. "I didn't mind. I've kind of come to expect it from folks around here, to be honest with you."

I hadn't realized that Emma had been taking such a beating around town about her decision to come back home to April Springs. "Has it really been that bad?"

"Don't worry about it. It's nothing I can't handle," Emma said. It was clear she didn't want to discuss it. Fine. If she changed her mind, she knew that I was always there for her.

"How do things stand in back?" I asked as I wiped down the last stretch of counter.

"We're nearly ready to close. If you balance the register, I can finish everything else up."

"That's a deal," I said.

I ran the reports I needed, counted the money in the till, and when I was finished, I was happy to have everything balance out perfectly. It wasn't that unusual to be off a nickel or so every now and then, but I loved it when everything worked out. It so rarely did in the life of a small businesswoman.

I was just finishing up the deposit slip when there was a knock at the front door. I looked up to see that Grace was standing there with a smile.

As I let her in, Emma came out from the back. "Suzanne, what should I do with the extra donuts today? Oh, hi, Grace."

"Hi right back at you," Grace said.

"How many are we talking about, Emma?" I asked.

"Two baker's dozens," she said.

I figured that twenty-six extra donuts wasn't that bad. "Do you have any use for them yourself?"

"Sorry," she said. "My mother's got Dad on a diet, and if I slip him any more goodies, I'm going to be in some serious trouble with her."

"We'll take them with us," Grace said suddenly.

"Feeling peckish, are you?" I asked her with a grin.

"What can I say? I'm still a growing girl." The statement was patently false, since Grace could still fit into her high school prom dress, but I let it go. I also knew that she wasn't about to eat all of those donuts, or probably even one.

Emma put the boxes on the counter, and then she said, "If that's it, I'll go ahead and take off. I've got a class in twenty minutes."

"Go on. Take off."

After she was gone, I asked Grace, "What are we going to do with all of these donuts? I know for a fact that *you're* not going to eat them."

"What we always do," Grace said. "We're going to use them to bribe people to talk to us. You don't mind, do you?"

"Are you kidding? I love that they might be going to good use, but I doubt that the DeAngelis ladies are going to want someone else's donuts around their restaurant."

"Then we'll use them on somebody else. Are you ready?"

"Let's drop my deposit off at the bank, and then I'm raring to go. I'll drive the Jeep so your car doesn't end up smelling like donuts."

"There are worse aromas in the world," she said, but she didn't disagree with my suggestion.

And just like that, we were off on another investigation.

Chapter 5

"Grace, there's something you should know," I said as I drove us to Union Square to visit Napoli's and the DeAngelis women, our sources there.

"Is it about the case?"

"Sort of. Jake is going to take some time off to help us solve it. That's not a problem, is it?"

"Why should it be?" she said. "I'm delighted."

"Good. I was afraid that you might not like him being a part of our team."

"Suzanne, I adore your boyfriend. Why wouldn't I want him around?"

I hesitated for a moment, and then I said, "Snooping is *our* thing, you know? I just didn't want you to feel left out."

"I'm here, aren't I? If Jake's helping us, where is he right now?"

"I have no idea. He said that he was going to try to tap into his official police sources for some inside information. In the meantime, we're going to keep each other up to speed about our progress, but unless something significant happens before then, we're meeting back at my house tonight for dinner. That reminds me," I said as I took out my phone and called my mother. "Hang on one second, Grace."

When my mother answered, I asked her, "Momma, would you mind making dinner for three unofficial investigators tonight?"

"I'd be delighted," she said. "Suzanne, you didn't drag George into this, did you?"

"No, ma'am, I realize that our mayor has enough on his hands without me adding to his problems. Jake is taking some vacation time to help us."

"Did he have any trouble getting leave on such short notice?"

"No, as a matter of fact, his boss was all for it," I said, not really sure if I was stretching the truth or not.

"Then that's perfect. Do you have any preferences about what's on the menu?"

"I'm sure that whatever you make will be splendid," I said, meaning every word of it. My mother was a fine cook, a savvy businesswoman, and a real pistol if anyone had the nerve to cross her. Not many did it twice; that was for sure.

"Give Grace my love. You two need to be careful, do you hear me?"

"Yes, ma'am," I said. "Loud and clear."

After I hung up, I told Grace, "Momma sends her love."

"Right back at her. How's she holding up?"

"You know my mother nearly as well as I do. I have a tough time reading her sometimes, but I can tell that she's pretty upset right now. Who can blame her? This is something no one would want dumped in their lap."

"Between the three of us, we'll figure this out," Grace said reassuringly.

"Don't forget that Chief Martin isn't exactly an innocent bystander in all of this. He wants this case solved as much as any of us. It can't be easy for him having his girlfriend as a prime murder suspect."

Grace glanced over at me. "Suzanne, if I didn't know any better, I'd say that you're becoming quite a fan of our dear police chief."

"He has his good points," I admitted. In all honesty, the chief really *had* started to win me over. No one that devoted to my mother could be all bad, and I was trying harder and harder to see him for what he was, and accept him.

I was willing to admit that some days were better than others, but it was good between us at the moment.

When Grace and I got to the restaurant, we found a sign on the door that said Napoli's was closed.

"What's going on?" Grace asked. "I thought they were open every lunchtime during the week."

"Me, too," I said as I grabbed my phone and called Angelica, the mother and patron saint of the best Italian restaurant I'd ever enjoyed.

"Angelica, this is Suzanne Hart. Are you okay?"

"I'm fine, Suzanne," she said rather abruptly. "Why do you ask?"

"Grace and I are out in front of the restaurant, and we just saw your sign that you were closed. I hope nothing's happened."

"I'm sorry to say that it has. Come around back. Hurry."

"If it's not a good time, we could always come back later." I felt bad asking her for a favor when she was clearly having trouble of her own.

"There's no time to talk. I'll be waiting."

Angelica hung up before I could protest any further.

"What's going on?" Grace asked.

"I don't have a clue, but we're about to find out." I led my friend around the back of the building. We had to knock twice on Napoli's rear entrance before anyone heard us. Sophia, Angelica's youngest, finally opened the door, a pained expression on her face. There was an expanding puddle of water at the base of the door, and I wondered if they'd had a rainstorm here that we'd missed in April Springs.

"What's the big mystery, Angelica?" I asked her.

"We've got a leak somewhere inside," she said as Grace and I walked into the kitchen.

A leak was the mildest way their problem could be described. A central pipe must have broken somewhere overhead, flooding the kitchen with at least six inches of water, and the tide was rising even as it came pouring out through the open back door. There were towels stacked up at the door that led to the main dining area, so I was hoping that the public spaces had been saved from the torrent of water. What made it worse was that there was the sound of more water coming in as Angelica, Antonia, and Maria tried to stem the tide, but they were clearly in a losing battle. The fourth daughter was nowhere to be found, but that didn't surprise me. Tianna had left the restaurant business abruptly over a boy that was sheer trouble, and sometimes Angelica was so distraught by it all that she claimed only three daughters, not four. I even caught myself on occasion forgetting about Tianna, but I hoped that someday she would come back into the fold. I knew that it must have broken Angelica's heart to lose contact with one of her children.

"Where's the cutoff valve for the main supply line?" I asked frantically.

"We don't know," Angelica said with great distraught. "I called our landlord, but he isn't picking up the phone. Everything's going to be ruined if we don't stop this water, and fast."

I looked around and tried to trace the exposed overhead plumbing, searching for some kind of cutoff valve. The only problem was that I couldn't find one. "How do you get up onto the roof?" I asked.

"I can't ask you to climb up there, Suzanne. Sophia, you go."

"I'm afraid of heights, and you know it."

"Just go!" her mother urged her, but she wouldn't move.

"I'll help you down here with a broom," Grace said as she started trying to push more water out the backdoor. It was clearly futile, but at least she was trying to do something.

"Come on, Sophia," I said as I grabbed her hand.

Once we were outside, I asked, "Can *you* think of any way to get up there?"

"I saw a ladder over there one time," she said as she pointed to a spot along the back wall, "but I'm not climbing up it. Suzanne, I wasn't kidding. I hate standing on a chair, let alone climbing around on a roof."

"Show me the ladder. I'll take care of the shutoff myself, but I have to be able to get up there first."

Sophia led me to the area she'd pointed to earlier, and there was indeed a ladder there, just as she'd promised. After taking a look at it, though, I wasn't at all certain that it was going to be tall enough for me to climb up onto the roof using it.

I grabbed it and leaned it against the building anyway. Just as I'd feared, it was a good two feet short of the roof.

"It's not going to work," Sophia said.

"I can climb it and pull myself up the rest of the way once I'm at the top," I answered. "Steady it for me, would you?"

I started climbing before I could chicken out. When I got to the top step, I reached up with both hands and pulled myself up the rest of the way. I managed to get my waist onto the edge, and then I pulled myself up. The T-shirt I was wearing was probably ruined by the hot tar on the lip of the roof, but I couldn't worry about that right now.

I had thought it was hot on the ground, but being up on that roof was a thousand times worse. Gravel that had once been embedded in hot tar was now loose and stuck to my shoes with every step I took. Hot exhausts from a dozen air conditioning units blew straight into my face, and I felt my feet grow heavier with every step.

I suddenly realized that I had to do this quickly if I was going to be able to do it at all.

Sophia yelled up, "Are you okay?"

"Walk to the restaurant's back door," I told her.

I started in the general direction, and as I looked over the edge, I saw Sophia standing there, shielding her eyes with one hand.

It was a great deal further up than I'd originally thought.

As I looked around the roof's maze of pipes, I found a plumbing stack with valves clustered together over to one side. This had to be where the leak was coming from. I grabbed the nearest valve and tried to turn it, but there were two problems with that: the valve was burning hot to the touch, and it was rusted a bit as well.

As I blew some air onto my fingertips to try to cool them off, I walked back and said, "I need a wrench."

"Sure, we've got one, but how am I going to get it up to you?"

"Don't worry, you don't have to climb up to let me have

it. You can throw it." That girl really was afraid of heights.

"Okay. I'll be back in a sec."

She took ten of them, and each one felt like a full minute apiece in the blistering heat.

Finally, Sophia reappeared. "Here it is."

"Throw it up," I said.

I'd planned on trying to catch it, but Sophia chucked it a little too hard, and it fumbled out of my hands.

"Sorry," she said.

"No worries," I answered.

I took the wrench, returned to the three valves, and with a little more effort, I shut them off one at a time. That most likely meant that I'd deprived two other businesses of their water as well, but let the landlord straighten it out.

I went back and found Sophia still standing there.

"See if that did the trick," I asked.

Sophia left my field of my vision, then she returned five seconds later.

"That did it," Sophia said. "The water stopped."

"Good," I answered as I walked back to where the ladder was.

It was further than I thought to that first rung when I looked down at it again.

I dropped the wrench to the ground, where it took an uncomfortable amount of time to fall, and then I shimmied my body over the side of the building and hoped that I'd be able to find the ladder with my feet. I could feel the tar and rocks of the roof bite into my hands, and my shoes were weighed down with tar and gravel, but I somehow managed to find the rung anyway.

After that, it was simply a matter of getting off that ladder as fast as I could and plant my feet firmly back onto the ground.

Sophia started to hug me as I stepped off onto the pavement, but I pushed her away. "Thanks, I appreciate the sentiment, but I'm a mess."

"Come into the restaurant. We'll take care of you."

I followed her back to Napoli's, stopping to take off my tennis shoes just before we got to the door. The shoes were a real mess, and I didn't want to track anything into Angelica's kitchen, as crazy as it must have seemed at the time, but I had to admit, that water felt good on my feet all the way through my socks.

Angelica took one look at me, and then she said with great distress, "Suzanne, you shouldn't have done that."

"I didn't mind," I said. "I know that you would have done it for me if the roles had been reversed. A friend in need and all of that."

"We'll make it right by you," she answered. "I promise."

"Don't worry about it, Angelica. This T-shirt was just about ready for the donation pile anyway, and my jeans didn't get very dirty."

"Where are your shoes, dear girl?" she asked me.

"I left them outside. I'll figure out a way to clean them up."

"Not even with a match and a can of gasoline," Sophia said. "They are worthless now."

"We'll replace them as well," Angelica said decisively, "but do any of you girls have extra shoes Suzanne can borrow in the meantime?"

That's when I remembered my running shoes in the back of the Jeep. "I've got another pair, but I really could use a clean shirt."

Maria dove into one of the boxes stored above the waterline and said, "Here's one of Napoli's best," she said.

"That's great," I answered as I took the pink shirt from her and looked at the restaurant's logo. Pink was by no means my color, but I wasn't about to be a choosy beggar.

Angelica wasn't about to leave it at that, though. "Ladies, surely we can do better than this."

"Not on such short notice we can't," Antonia answered.

"Then we must focus on the long term." Angelica turned to me and said, "I wish I could offer you something to eat, but it's difficult to run a restaurant without running water."

"I could always go turn it back on, if you'd like," I said with the hint of a smile. Just being around these strong women made me feel better.

"No!" three of them shouted at the same time.

"Then Grace and I will take a rain check," I said.

Angelica said, "Girls, let's get busy. I want to open as soon as the water is restored."

"We're going to need a ton of fans to dry the place out," Maria said.

"Then go to the hardware store and tell Henry that we need them. He'll lend us everything we need."

"And come himself if there's a chance of seeing you," Sophia answered.

"Is there something going on that I don't know about?" I asked. I knew of only one man Angelica had dated in the past few years, and that had come to a rather abrupt and tragic end. Was she back in the dating pool?

"It's all nonsense," Angelica said, though her color rose slightly. "Henry and I are just friends."

"You may feel that way," Sophia said, "but I guarantee you that Henry doesn't. That man wants more than just your lasagna," she said with a grin.

Angelica whipped a towel at her. "You may go with your sister, or stay here and work. You choose."

Sophia was out the door behind Maria quicker than I'd ever seen her move.

Once they were gone, Angelica told her remaining daughter, "Let's get busy making this place fit again."

As they began to work, Grace and I started to join in.

"I won't hear of it. You've done enough," Angelica said.

"We've got the time," I said, "and we're happy to help."

Angelica wasn't buying that, though. "Was there something else you wanted besides a meal?"

"I did at first, but it can wait."

"Suzanne Hart, talk to me." I knew that tone of voice, especially since I'd heard it from Momma enough times. Angelica wasn't fooling around. She wanted to return my recent favor, and if I knew what was good for me, I'd let her.

"We need to know about two men who used to live in Union Square a long time ago, before I was born," I said.

"Any two in particular?" she asked.

"The Briar boys, Morgan and Blake," I said.

Angelica frowned, and then she said, "I'll tell you what I know, but I should warn you, none of it is good."

A sudden question burst forth in my mind. "Angelica, did you ever meet my father when he lived here in town? He was separated from my mother at the time."

The expression on Angelica's face was enough to tell me that I'd scored a direct hit. Grace was astonished as well, but I'd have to bring her up to speed later.

"We'll discuss this outside," she said, clearly to Antonia's displeasure.

"You don't have time to tell me about it now," I said, suddenly not at all sure that I wanted to hear what she had to say. "This can wait."

"I've wanted to tell you for many years. I won't let another opportunity pass," Angelica said as we walked outside.

Grace, sensing the tone of the coming conversation, said, "I'll stay and help Antonia."

Antonia looked pleased by the news, but not as happy as I was. I'd share everything I learned with Grace later, but for now, I needed to hear what Angelica had to say all by myself.

Chapter 6

"So, tell me the truth. Did you know my dad?"

"I did," Angelica said, though it was clear that she wasn't all that happy talking about it all these years later.

A thought suddenly struck me. "You didn't *date* him, did you?"

"Of course not. Remember, I was happily married back then. Besides, the entire time your father lived in Union Square, as far as I knew he never looked at another woman, let alone dated anyone. He was loyal to your mother, for what it was worth."

"If they didn't split up over someone else, why did they break up, then?"

"Suzanne, you were married once. You know the ebb and flow most marriages go through. You shouldn't be too hard on your father. He had his reasons, I'm sure."

"I wish someone would enlighten me about what exactly they were," I said a little too harshly.

"If that's what you're hoping to find out, then I'm afraid that I won't be of any use to you," Angelica said as she started back inside.

I reached out and touched her arm lightly. "I'm sorry. I didn't mean to take it out on you. It's just so frustrating, knowing that there was this entire chapter in my parents' lives that I didn't ever know happened."

"It was before you were born, so I can understand why your mother didn't want to bring it up. I'm willing to wager that if Morgan Briar hadn't come to April Springs, she *never* would have told you."

"How did you know?"

"Word spreads quickly. I shouldn't have to tell you that."

It was true. I'd seen the speed of the grapevine firsthand before. "Why did he choose this past week to come visit us?"

I asked. "His brother died a long time ago. So why show up now looking to blackmail us?"

"You didn't know?"

"Know what?" I asked.

"He had a very good reason for waiting this long. You see, Morgan Briar just got out of jail."

"What was the charge?" I asked.

"That I thought you knew. He tried to kill your father the day after someone ran down his brother, and from what I heard, he was just released a few days ago."

"He tried to kill my dad?" I asked in disbelief. If Morgan had succeeded, then there would have been no me. The thought of it made me a little queasy. "What happened?"

"It was Morgan's idea of an eye for an eye. He waited for your father to come out of a diner downtown, and then he tried to run him down. The man was obsessed; he didn't care who saw it. He was out for what he thought of as revenge."

"Did he miss Dad altogether?"

"No, he actually clipped his leg with the bumper of his car. The metal caught his flesh, and he must have had a pretty substantial scar from it for the rest of his life."

"He told me once that a shark bit him," I said, remembering my father's effort to make a joke of the scar. "I never asked him what really happened. Still, over thirty years is a long time to serve for just *attempting* to kill someone."

"It would have been if Morgan had kept his nose clean, but he was always getting into trouble in jail. Frankly, I'm amazed they *ever* let him out."

"How do you know so much about all of this?" I asked. "Surely it's not common knowledge in Union Square."

"You'd be surprised. After all, it's a small town. Plus, his sister is still around, and she's kept me up to date over the years. You could always speak to her yourself, if you'd like."

"What are the chances that she'd give me the time of day, seeing how our families are locked in some kind of bizarre feud? She probably blames Dad for one brother's death, and my mother or me for the other."

"Let me call her and see how she feels about you approaching her," Angelica said.

"You don't have to do that. It's too much to ask."

"Like climbing up on a roof for a friend?" she asked with a slight smile.

"That was different," I protested.

"Yes, it was. All I'm doing is making a simple telephone call. You actually put yourself in harm's way for me and my family."

"I don't see it that way at all," I said.

"I'm not at all surprised that you don't. Suzanne, let me do this for you."

"Okay," I conceded. "I really do appreciate it. This makes us even."

"Not on your life," Angelica said with a smile, and then she stepped away to make her call. In the meantime, Maria and Sophia came back, carrying two box fans apiece.

"What did you do, wipe him out?" I asked them.

"We did," Maria said proudly. "He would have given us more if he'd had them."

"My mother has that man wrapped around her little finger," Sophia said. Evidently she thought that she'd spoken softly enough not to be overheard, but there was a sudden sharp cough from Angelica's direction, and we all hurried inside to set the fans up.

The water was mostly out of the kitchen, either through the mops or the doorway we'd just stepped through, and Antonia set up the fans where they would do the most good. I had a hunch the kitchen would be dry in no time, and if the dining area had been spared, Napoli's most likely would be open for dinner tonight.

We were all using towels to get the last of the water up when a short, balding man with a big pear-shaped belly stormed in. "Have you people lost your minds? Who turned off the water to every tenant in the complex?" he asked with a growl.

"That would be me," I said calmly as I stepped forward. There was no way that I was going to let anyone else take the blame for me.

"Well, what's the big idea? The other businesses need their water." The fact that I was so calm was evidently throwing him off a little.

"If you'd come here when I first called," Angelica said as she came into the kitchen, "we wouldn't have had to take such drastic measures. I expect that pipe to be fixed, and I mean in half an hour."

"That's crazy. I can't get someone to come out on such short notice," he said.

"Okay, I'm a reasonable woman," Angelica said. "I'll give you a *full* hour. If we don't have running water by then, I'm charging you for what I've lost in revenue today."

"You can bill me all that you want to, but I'm not paying you one dime. That's what insurance is for."

"No," Angelica said softly. "That's what my cousins are for. Now, are you going to settle this with me, or should I tell them to come over right now and help you change your mind?"

"I'll see what I can do," the landlord said as he grabbed his phone, walked outside, and quickly started dialing.

"Why is he so afraid of your cousins?" I whispered. "Has he even met them?"

Angelica peeked outside, and then she closed the door for a moment. "I don't *have* any cousins, but somehow he got the idea that we're connected in some way."

"Connected? What does that mean?" I asked naively.

"You know, connected," she said as she put an index finger on the side of her nose.

"The Mafia?" I asked loudly. I never would have believed that could ever be true, not even if Angelica herself told me.

"Keep your voice down," she said with a smile. "I never said a word to the man, but he assumed that just because we're Italian, we're trouble."

"We are," Sophia said, "but in a very different way than

he believes."

"And you never set him straight?" I asked.

"I tried half a dozen times, but he never believed me. Anyway, it has served its purpose over the years. If it gets me service that he might not ordinarily offer to his regular tenants, who does it hurt?"

I didn't even know how to respond to that, and fortunately I was saved from trying when Angelica's phone rang. She answered it, held a brief whispered conversation, and then jotted something down on a Napoli's notepad.

After she hung up, Angelica handed me a folded note.

"Suzanne, you'll find everything that you need right there," she said. "Go on. It's all taken care of."

"What's taken care of?" Sophia asked.

"Nosy Rosie's latest membership list," Angelica said as she winked at me, and then she turned to her daughters. "Girls, thank Suzanne and Grace for their help."

The women acted much younger than they really were, all saying in nearly perfect unison, "Thank you, Suzanne and Grace."

Angelica just laughed as she looked at me. "I'm afraid that's the best that you're going to get from the likes of these three."

"Honestly, it's more than we need," I said, and as Grace and I left the kitchen, I added, "By the way, you're all most welcome."

The second we were back in the Jeep, Grace said, "I've been dying to ask you something since you came back in. What did I miss out there in that hushed conversation you had with Angelica?"

"More than I can catch you up on in twenty minutes," I said.

"At least give me the highlights," she answered.

I took a deep breath, and then I decided to tell Grace everything that I knew. "Dad lived here when he and Mom were separated a long time ago. Angelica knew him, but they never dated. Dad had some trouble with the Briar brothers, and when Blake was run over, Morgan tried to kill my father. He went to prison, and he just got out. That's when he came gunning for us."

"Wow," Grace said with clear admiration. "That was incredible the way you summarized that so quickly. Was Angelica able to give us any leads?"

"She did something better than that. She set up an interview for us with Blake and Morgan's sister," I said as I opened the note.

I wasn't sure what address I was expecting, a residential street somewhere perhaps.

Instead, it said, "Go to the police station and ask for Ellen."

Evidently our investigation was going to begin in one of the oddest places that I'd ever expected to be hunting for a killer.

But truthfully, not by all that much.

"Are you Ellen?" I asked the woman behind the desk at police headquarters when Grace and I walked in. The officer sitting there was in uniform, and her graying hair was pulled back in a rather severe bun. From the look in her eyes, she clearly hadn't gotten that much sleep the night before.

"Is that supposed to be some kind of joke?" she asked.

"No, of course not. I really was told to come here and ask for a woman named Ellen."

"I'm not talking about you. Ask your friend if she's trying to be funny coming in here like that."

I'd nearly forgotten that Grace was behind me carrying two boxes crammed full of donuts. "Sorry, that's my fault. My name is Suzanne Hart. I own the donut shop in April Springs, and I thought you all might like a treat. I wasn't trying to imply anything about cops and donuts, honest I wasn't. It's a good will gesture, nothing more." That wasn't entirely true. What it had been was a way to ingratiate us with local law enforcement, and maybe get on this woman's good side.

"Okay," she said as her frown eased. "There are just too many jokes going around about cops and donuts, you know what I mean? I'm sure everyone will appreciate them." She took the boxes from Grace and slid them onto the counter beside her. "I knew who you were the second you walked in here, and I didn't need the donuts as a hint. It's pretty clear that you're the woman Angelica called me about," she added as she pointed to my shirt.

I'd forgotten all about the T-shirt I'd borrowed from the crew at Napoli's. "Sorry about that. I needed something clean in a hurry."

"It's not a problem," Ellen said as she stared at me for a full second, and then she added, "So, Thomas Hart was your dad."

"He was," I said. "I'm sorry for your loss. Actually, I'm kind of surprised that you came into work today after what happened last night."

She sighed, and then Ellen offered a weak shrug. "There was nothing I could do at home, and the quiet there was driving me crazy. Morgan could be a real thorn in my side since I'm a cop and he'd been in jail for what seemed like forever, but he swore that he'd changed in prison, and I'd been looking forward to getting to know him all over again. Somebody owes me for that, you know?"

"I promise you that neither my mother nor I had anything to do with what happened to your brother last night."

Ellen didn't seem to be all that impressed with my word of honor. "I understand that the chief of police is investigating the murder," she said.

"He's a good man," I answered. "He'll find your brother's killer."

"If you believe that, then why are you and your friend digging into Morgan's death?"

"What have you heard?" I asked. Normally, folks I just met didn't come right out and ask such a blunt question about my unofficial investigations with Grace.

"Angelica and I go way back. She told me exactly why you wanted to talk to me." Ellen looked at her watch, and then she added, "My relief is waiting in the wings, hoping I'll take some time off to give her some time behind the desk. Why not give her the chance to earn some of her pay today?" Ellen turned and called out to a much younger woman. "Denise, I need a break. I'll be back in five."

As the new officer approached us, she said, "Take your time, ma'am. I've got it covered."

Ellen didn't smile. "Like I said, five minutes should do it."

As the three of us walked out of the precinct to a row of benches in front of the station, Ellen said, "That woman has been itching to replace me since she got here last month straight out of the academy."

"That kind of enthusiasm can be draining, can't it?" Grace said with a weary smile.

"Oh, yes," Ellen said as she looked at Grace. "That sounds like the voice of experience."

"I've got someone under me who's dying to move me out," she admitted.

"How are you handling it?" Ellen asked.

"Let's just say that for the moment, I'm keeping her busy with things she'd rather not be doing. Sooner or later, she'll either quit, or she'll learn about cause and effect."

"I wish I could do something like that, but I don't have the authority to set up her work schedule."

"Sorry about that."

"No reason to be sorry; it's not your fault," Ellen said, and then she turned to me. "I should tell you up front that I don't approve of civilians getting involved in active police investigations."

"Neither does my boyfriend, usually," I said.

"Excuse me for saying so, but why should I care what your boyfriend thinks, one way or the other?"

"Normally you shouldn't, but he happens to be a special investigator for the state police."

Ellen looked surprised by my claim. "And he doesn't mind this time?"

"Not only that, he's taking vacation time to help us out," I said.

The officer looked around as she asked, "If he's working with you two, then where is he right now?"

"He's following up on other leads."

Ellen thought about that, and then she shrugged. "Fine. There was a reason besides friendship that I agreed to see you. You spoke with my brother not long before he was murdered. What did he want to talk to you about?"

Could I just blurt out that he'd been trying to blackmail me after what the woman had just told us about his promise to reform? Then again, did I have the gall to lie to her about something so important? In the end, I decided that, no matter how painful it might be for her to hear, she deserved the truth. "He was trying to blackmail me. I'm sorry."

Ellen looked as though she might cry, but after a moment, it passed. "You weren't responsible for it, and on the face of it, neither was I. I wish I could say that finding out that my brother's promises to me were lies surprises me, but I have to admit that I'm not all that shocked. Go ahead, you might as well give it all to me in one pop."

I explained his blackmail plan to Ellen, and she interrupted me before I could finish. "What proof did he have that your father was responsible for Blake's death?"

"The main thing was a letter my father wrote to Blake just before he died. He was angry with your brother, and he threatened him."

She thought about that for a few seconds, and then she asked, "And you saw this letter with your own eyes?"

"Not me," I said, and after taking a deep breath, I added, "He showed it to my mother."

"She was with you at the donut shop when Morgan approached you?"

"No," I said. "The two of them spoke later."

"Let me guess," Ellen said. "My brother tried to put the

touch on her as well."

"That's what it sounded like to me."

"How did your mother react?"

"She told him that she wouldn't be blackmailed. Then she slapped him and she stormed off," I said, feeling a twinge of pride in my mother, knowing what the outburst must have cost her.

"Or so she says," Ellen said.

"I don't have any reason to doubt her," I insisted.

"Relax, I'm not accusing her of anything."

It was time for me to ask a question. "Did Morgan say *anything* to you about what he was up to?"

"I may be working a desk at the station, but I'm just as much a cop as any detective on the police force is." It was clear that she had a bit of a chip on her shoulder about that.

"I wasn't implying anything. I just thought that blood might be thicker than water."

"No way. The force is more of a family than my brother ever was to me. Just because I let him bunk in my spare room didn't mean that I was willing to put up with any of his foolishness. If Morgan were still alive, I'd throw him out on his ear right now. He didn't even make it a week out of prison, six lousy days was all that he had on the outside before he got in trouble again."

"He was staying with you?" I asked. "Is there any way that we could look through his things? I know it must sound ghoulish, but it might help us find out who killed him."

"Your Chief Martin already searched his room, and so did I."

I wasn't all that surprised that the chief had inspected Morgan's room before we could get to it. Despite our past differences, I believed that the man was a good cop who just got in over his head sometimes. "Did either one of you find anything significant?" I asked.

"That I'm willing to tell you? No."

"We understand how you must feel," Grace said. "We're just trying to help."

"Did they search his computer?" I asked.

"Morgan was a real Luddite. He hated the things, and he wouldn't know how to turn one on, let alone use it for anything."

"What if he needed something done that used a computer?" I asked.

"Morgan was big on finding people who did things *for* him. He was proud that no matter what the situation, he 'knew a guy' who could take care of whatever he needed for him. It was all very old school behavior." Ellen looked from me to Grace, and then back at me again. "Ladies, I may not approve of what you're doing, but I understand your motivation."

"Is there any place that your brother liked to hang out?" I asked. "Can you give us *anything*?"

Ellen shook her head. "I wish that I could, but Morgan mostly kept to himself. Sorry."

"That's okay," I said. "Again, I truly am sorry for your loss. I didn't care for your brother, but he didn't deserve to die that way."

"I just wish that I could believe that," Ellen said after a moment's pause, "but I'm afraid that he might have gotten *exactly* what he had coming to him in the end."

CRESCENT EXPRESS

These aren't necessarily what you expect when you think of donuts, but I love playing with doughs stocked in the freezer section of our grocery store. I made crescent rolls for our family dinner one night, and thought, why not deep-fry these? It took some work to get them just right, but I'm happy enough with the instructions to share them now. You have to fry these well past the appearance of them being finished, and the crust is definitely a darker shade of brown than you'd expect if you were baking them. For another option, you could bake them in your oven just as you normally would, but keep the fillings. We especially like the bits of melted chocolate goodness in the chocolate version.

INGREDIENTS

Crescent roll dough, 1 can (I like the 8 oz. pack)

Canola Oil for frying (the amount depends on your pot or fryer)

ADDITIONS

The space to add fillings inside the crescent roll is small, so don't get too carried away! A tiny amount, around 2 teaspoons, is usually enough. Some of our fillings include cut strawberry pieces, dehydrated pineapple chunks, fresh apple bits, and even mini semi-sweet chocolate chips!

INSTRUCTIONS

This couldn't be simpler. Start the oil heating, then open and unroll the crescent dough. Add the filling of your choice, roll up as usual, but be sure to pinch the ends so the filling doesn't escape during frying. If baking, see the directions for the proper length of time and temperature (375 degrees F for 10-12 minutes works for me). If you are frying, cook in hot Canola oil (360 to 370 degrees F) 1 1/2 to 3 minutes, turning halfway through. This is an art-form, and may take some time to get just right. The first time I did this, I started taking them out at 1 1/2 minutes, and then every thirty seconds until I was satisfied with the result!

Yield 8 Crescent Expresses

Chapter 7

"Well, that was a whole lot of useless," Grace said after Ellen went back inside the police station. "I was hoping for more."

"Grace, you know as well as I do that not every lead we get is a solid one. Morgan had to be doing *something* besides trying to blackmail my family in the six days since he was out of prison."

"You're right, but how are we possibly going to learn what he was doing?"

"Well, we can start by looking under every rock in Union Square that we can find," I said as I glanced at my watch. "But not today. I need to get home and clean up before Jake comes over."

"I just wish that we had something good to share with him," Grace said.

"I feel as though we've made a good start," I said. "Don't forget, this is just the beginning of our investigation."

"Well, we can't take too long. There's too much at stake."

"I agree with you, but we're doing the best we can," I said. "Let's just hope that Jake had more luck than we did today."

Judging by the vehicle already pulled into my driveway, my boyfriend was already waiting for us at home when we got there. So much for sneaking in and getting cleaned up before he could see me in the rough shape that I was currently in. I'd done my best to repair the damage from my time on the roof at Napoli's, but I knew that I hadn't been all that successful when I looked in the Jeep's rearview mirror before I got out.

"Do you want to go my place and grab a quick shower there?" Grace asked. "You've still got a change of clothes over there, remember?"

I'd forgotten all about leaving clothes there, though I remembered Grace's outfit in my closet upstairs. "That would be great," I said as I readjusted my mirror, only to see Jake standing behind the Jeep with a huge grin on his face.

"Thanks, but it appears that it's too late for that now," I said as I got out.

Jake kissed me soundly after wrapping me up in his arms. "Hey, stranger," he said. "I've missed you."

"I'm a mess," I said as I tried to at least tuck my hair behind my ears.

"Really? You look beautiful to me," he said.

"Now I know that you're a big fat liar," I said. "I look dreadful, and I fully realize just how much I desperately need a shower right now."

Jake released me and then he took a step back, looking me over from head to toe. "Lady, you need to replace that defective mirror of yours, because I don't know what you've been looking at."

Grace laughed. "If I didn't know it before, I realize it now. This one's a keeper, Suzanne."

"That's what *I* keep telling her," Jake said with a laugh. He was in an extremely good mood, and I hope that my company had something to do with it.

From the front door, Momma asked, "Are you three going to stand out there gabbing all evening, or does anyone want to eat?" Then she got a closer look at me. "Suzanne Hart, have you been crawling around in the dirt?"

"Just the opposite, as a matter of fact," I said with a smile.

"I don't even know what that's supposed to mean," Momma said with a cryptic look on her face.

"I was on the roof over at Napoli's this afternoon," I admitted.

"What were you doing up there?" Jake asked.

"It's a long story. Momma, do I have time to take a shower before we eat?"

"Even if you didn't, I'd find a way to *make* the time. By

all means, go clean yourself up."

I kissed her cheek. "Thanks."

"You're welcome. In the meantime, I'll entertain your guests."

"Why don't you sing for them?" I suggested.

"What?" she asked.

"Well, I know that I'd personally find that pretty entertaining," I answered with a grin.

"Oh, go on," she said.

I turned to Jake. "Can our updates wait until after we eat dinner?"

"As a matter of fact, I'd prefer it," he said.

I thanked him, and then, as I disappeared upstairs to clean myself up, I paused a moment to take it all in. I felt loved by everyone gathered there. I didn't have any siblings, but Grace was better than any sister I could have ever imagined, and though Momma was stern and could be tough at times, she was perfectly suited to me. As for Jake, *whenever* I was with him, I felt as though I belonged.

Family could be gathered together at any time, in any place, and bloodlines had nothing to do it. What mattered most was that there was love, and safety, and acceptance, all around me.

Murder might have been the cause of the get-together, but it didn't detract from the spirit of love that existed in my home.

"Oh, that's much better," Momma said as I came downstairs after a quick shower and a change into clean clothes. I'd had to scrub rather hard at a spot on my elbow that the asphalt had marked, but it had finally come clean, too.

"I don't know what you're talking about. I think she looked great before," Jake said.

"That's just because you're hungry," Grace said. "Susanne, your mother wouldn't let him eat until you were back downstairs with us."

"Grace Gauge, you *know* that's not true," Momma said.

"I even offered him a snack while we waited."

"I'm just teasing you," Grace said as she hugged my mother. Momma had stepped in when Grace's parents had died years ago, and the two of them had a close relationship in their own right that had nothing to do with me.

Jake added, "Besides, I wasn't about to dull my appetite with cheese and crackers when I knew what was on the menu."

"What are we having?" I asked Momma as we walked into the dining room. No surprise, she'd set the table with some of her formal china. Any meal could be an event with my mother, after all.

"Nothing all that special. I just threw something together," she said with a grin.

I smelled the air, and caught the unmistakable aroma of her pot roast. "Wow, that is heavenly."

"I found a new recipe for slow cooking a roast in one of my mysteries," my mother said with a grin.

"Well, I can't wait to try it," Jake said.

"Please, everyone sit. I'll be right back."

"Do you need any help in the kitchen?" I offered.

"No, thank you. I'm fine."

After Momma was in the kitchen, Jake looked at me and asked, "Does she usually get her recipes from mystery novels? Not that I'm complaining, but it seems like a rather odd combination to me."

"Culinary mysteries are a strong niche in the cozy field she loves," I said. The only reason I'd known that was because of the lecture I'd been given on the same topic from Momma when she'd switched from craft-related cozies to her current trend of reading what she called foodies. She'd even read a series based on a donut shop, of all things. I'd picked one up once to browse through, but I usually don't check out too many mysteries myself. I had to admit that the recipes looked pretty good, though, and I thought about trying a few for my customers the next time I was searching for something new to offer my clientele at Donut Hearts.

After we gave thanks for the meal, Momma dished out our plates. The roast was so tender it fell apart at first contact with my fork, and I could smell the bay leaves and thyme as I dished a little of the gravy onto it. The carrots were perfect, and the tiny new potatoes popped open like gifts to receive the butter I added. This wasn't the time to skimp on the extras, and I was a true fan of real butter, not some oleo substitute chock full of chemicals.

Taking a small serving of each offering, I put the forkful of food in my mouth and the flavors exploded. After I dispatched the first bite, I said, "I don't know how your mystery was, but this recipe is fantastic."

"I told you that my habit of reading mysteries would come in handy someday," she said.

I turned to Jake, and I saw a substantial smile on his face. "What do you think?"

After a second, he looked at me and asked, "Did you say something? I was just thinking that this is probably the best thing I've ever eaten in my life."

Grace echoed the thought as well, and Momma grinned as she said, "Don't fill up on pot roast. I know that it's good, but I made dessert as well."

"What are we having?" I asked, and then I took another bite of roast and carrot.

"Suzanne, how can you even *think* about dessert when we're eating *this* masterpiece?" Jake asked me.

"I want to see if there's any reason *not* to eat this until I can't move."

"It's chocolate explosion pie," Momma said.

"Well?" Grace asked. "What are you going to do?"

My Momma's pies were famous in our parts, but it was still a coin toss. After some thought, I finally said, "I might back off the pot roast a little, and then have a sliver of pie, too."

"Wow, that must be some pie," Jake said.

"Try it yourself, and then see if I'm selling it short."

"Suzanne, when it comes to food, I'm going to take your

word for it every time. I can hardly wait."

The pie was just as delicious as I imagined that it would be, though I limited myself to a small slice, at least the first time I sampled some. The second slice was a little bigger, but in my defense, the combined slices were still less than I usually had in one helping.

"I'm now officially too stuffed to move," I said as I pushed the dessert plate away, nearly polished clean from my attack on the pie.

"Why don't you all go into the living room, and I'll clean up?" Momma suggested.

We all protested at the same time, but my mother wasn't a woman who would allow her suggestions to be vetoed. "You are here to discuss the current state of your investigation, am I correct?"

There were three nods, and then she continued, "I'm making myself useful in the best way I know how, and you should as well. Everyone needs to go into the living room and solve this dreadful man's murder. After all, that's what the three of *you* are best at. Now, are there any more arguments?"

As I'd expected, there were none, and Momma looked satisfied with our silence.

Jake took one side of the couch, and I joined him there, while Grace sat in the chair I usually occupied.

"Actually, I don't have all that much to say," Jake began. "I spent the afternoon in Union Square."

"So did we," I said. "Why didn't we see you there?"

"Well, I was at police headquarters most of the time," Jake said.

"We were there, too," Grace replied.

"I didn't know that. Why didn't I see you there?"

"Where exactly were you?" I asked.

"I was back in the detective bullpen talking to a guy named Gravely. Why? Where were you two?"

"We were talking to the dispatcher up front," I said.

"The older officer with her hair in a bun? I believe that

her name was Ellen."

I looked at him in amazement. "What was her social security number?"

"I don't have a clue," Jake admitted, looking quite perplexed by the question. "Why on earth should I know that?"

"I was just curious, since you seemed to know everything *else* about her." I paused, and then added, "Well, maybe not *everything*."

"I don't follow you," Jake said, clearly confused by the turn this conversation was taking. You'd have thought that he would have been used to it by now, after being with me.

"That officer just happens to be the third Briar sibling."

"I had no idea," he said in astonishment.

"Don't beat yourself up about it. We had help. Angelica DeAngelis told us."

"I suppose that ties into your earlier statement that you were climbing around on Napoli's roof. Care to elaborate on that?"

"I thought we were taking turns," I said.

"I'll cede the floor in this instance," Jake answered.

"I had to shut off the water," I said.

"On the roof?"

"It turned out that it was for some kind of fire extinguishing system," I said, having finally found that out as I was leaving.

"And *you* were the only one who could have done it," Jake said.

"Well, Angelica, Antonia, Maria and Grace were cleaning up, and Sophia's afraid of heights."

"Is that supposed to be an explanation?" he asked me.

"I don't know *how* I could say it any clearer. Angelica is our source of information when it comes to Union Square, so we went to Napoli's. We found their flood disaster in progress when we got there, and I figured the investigation could wait. A friend needed us, and we responded."

"I would have expected nothing less from either one of

you," he said. "Did you have any luck with the Briar sibling?"

"Not much," I admitted. "Morgan got out of prison six days ago and the first thing he did was move in with Ellen. He promised her that he'd turned over a new leaf, but clearly that wasn't the case. We asked if we could search his room, but she declined. We don't have any official status in the investigation, and she wouldn't budge."

"Maybe I could talk to her tomorrow," Jake suggested.

"You can try," Grace said, "but we already dropped your name, and although she was a little impressed that you were helping us, it didn't win her over completely."

"You dropped my name?" he asked.

"She didn't; I did. I didn't think you'd mind. Do you?" I asked. If Jake was going to work with us, he couldn't be ashamed that we were amateurs, especially with our track record of solving murders together.

"Not one bit," he said hastily. The man was learning my tone of voice pretty quickly, something that I was thankful for. It would probably save us *both* some aggravation down the road. I, too, was learning the way he thought, and how to read his tone of voice and his expressions, something I'd never been able to manage with Max, the Great Impersonator, even after all the years that we'd known each other. Jake added, "I still think that I should talk to her tomorrow. Cops talk to each other in a different language, you know?"

"Hey, you're welcome to give it a try," I said. "Like I said, we didn't uncover much of anything."

"Don't sell yourselves short," he said. "I think you both did an exemplary job with what little information you had to go on."

"Thanks," I said. "So, what were you able to come up with?"

"Actually, I was lucky enough to see the files of the original hit-and-run," he said. "Suzanne, do you really need to know everything about what I uncovered?"

"Are you asking me if I can I take you telling me things

about my father that I really don't want to know? Is that the real question, Jake?"

"It is, and I want you to think hard about your answer before you say anything."

"I don't have to," I said firmly. "I know that neither of my parents have ever been saints. Tell me what you uncovered, and then leave it up to me to deal with it."

I looked toward the kitchen, and I saw that the door was slightly ajar. Had it been an accident, or was Momma listening in on our conversations? I'd just as soon think that she'd been eavesdropping; it would save me from explaining it all to her again later, and I meant what I'd said. If I could hear it, so could she.

"It appears that your father drank quite a bit while he lived in Union Square. The 'Jack' nickname came from his favorite drink, Jack Daniel's, straight up."

"So what? I never dreamed that my father was ever a teetotaler."

"You don't understand. He drank until he passed out on more than one occasion, at least according to the eyewitness reports at the time."

My father as town drunk was not a role that I'd ever imagined him playing, but it was well before I was born, so I had no right to judge him. "Did the cops at the time think that he might have killed Blake Briar?"

"One might have, but the rest of them realized that there were no conspiracies there. If your father hadn't reported his car stolen two days *before* the accident, it might have been a different story."

"Is the cop still around who *didn't* believe him?"

"He's still on the force, as a matter of fact. I'm seeing him tomorrow, along with Ellen Briar. I have a hunch that Morgan's murder had more to do with the past than what's happened since he's been out of jail. I've got a few more angles on Blake Briar's death that I still need to follow up."

"Like what?" I asked, fascinated by just how good a cop my boyfriend really was. He'd already started applying his special talents to this case, and I was glad to have him on our side.

"I'm going to the prison in the next day or two to interview some of the staff there. If anyone else got out recently, or even had a major grudge against Morgan, I'll uncover it. I'm especially interested to see if he ever talked about his brother while he was in there."

"That's great and all," Grace said, "but what are we supposed to do in the meantime? It seems like you're covering *all* of the bases."

I hadn't said it, but I'd been thinking it, too. I just hoped that I didn't have to admit it to Jake.

No such luck, though.

He turned to me with a troubled expression as he asked, "Suzanne, do you feel that way, too?"

"It *does* seem as though you've got the complete investigation under control," I admitted.

Jake ran a hand through his hair before he answered. "I wish I had your faith in me. As a matter of fact, there's a ton of stuff that I *can't* do."

"We're not too good to work on crumbs," I said.

"Let's see, where should we start? Morgan was out of jail for six days. What else was he up to? Did he have a girlfriend? How about drinking buddies? Had he looked for a job in the time he was out? There are a thousand questions you can ask around Union Square that I'd have a hard time getting answers to as a cop."

"But how do we find the right people to talk to?" Grace asked.

Jake just shrugged. "That's part of the joy of police work. It can be a slow grind, but it's the best shot we've got. Listen, if I'm doing too much, all you have to do is say so, and I'll back off. Are you both sure that you're okay with me working on this case with you?"

"Yes," Grace and I said in unison.

"Okay, because the last thing I want is to alienate either one of you." Jake stretched, and then said, "If you don't mind, I'm going to hit the hay."

"Are you staying with Cam again?" I asked. Cam Jennings rented rooms on an extremely selective basis, something he did for the company more than the paltry additional income it provided him.

"Yes, he was happy to have me, even on such short notice. I'm going to head over there right now and prepare my notes so I'll be ready for tomorrow."

As Jake stood, I joined him, and kissed him soundly before he could go.

"Not that I'm complaining, but what was that for?" he asked.

"For taking this just as seriously as you do your regular job," I said.

Grace stood and kissed his cheek. "That's *my* way of thanking you."

Just then, Momma walked into the living room, but I knew that her timing was no coincidence. She had two small parcels wrapped in aluminum foil, and she handed them both to Jake as she approached him. "You have my thanks, as well," she said, and then on the spur of the moment, she kissed his cheek on the other side of Grace's peck.

"If I knew about the rewards I'd get helping you out, I'd have done it long ago," he said with a grin.

"We know what this is costing you," I said. "We just want to be sure that you know how much we appreciate it." I turned to Grace and I said, "I'm going to walk him out, but if you'll stick around, I'd love to chat a little more."

Grace nodded. "That sounds good to me." Then she looked at Momma and asked, "Is there *any* chance there's pie left?"

"Of course," Momma answered with a grin. She loved requests for seconds and thirds, and she treated them as the applause they represented.

"Hey, save some for me," I protested.

"That depends on how long it takes you to get back here," Grace said.

"Bye, Jake," I said with a smile.

"No, ma'am. *You're* coming with me."

He tugged at my hand, but I needed no prompting at all.

Outside at his car, I said, "I really am glad that you're here."

"I am, too," he said, and then he kissed me one last time. "I hate to ask your mother to feed us again tomorrow so that we can catch up again. Should I take us all out to dinner instead?"

"Where do you suggest we go? There's no place in town or anywhere nearby where we can have the privacy to talk about these cases openly. Besides, do you honestly *want* to break my mother's heart? She's probably poring over recipes for tomorrow night even as we speak."

"Well, I wouldn't want to hurt her feelings," he said with a grin.

"Good, then it's settled. See you tomorrow evening. Be careful, Jake."

"Right back at you, Suzanne. Good night."

"Night," I said, and after he was gone, I hurried back inside.

After all, I found that I suddenly had room for another sliver of pie myself, and I wanted to make sure that I got one in time before it was all gone.

Chapter 8

Oh happy day.

There was enough pie left for me when I got back inside. I grabbed a fork and the last piece, and then I joined Momma and Grace at the kitchen table.

After I took my first bite, I turned to my mother and smiled as I said, "Don't even try to pretend that you didn't hear every word we spoke," I said as I pointed my empty fork at her.

"I wouldn't dream of it," Momma answered. "And don't point at me, young lady, not even with a fork. Jake is quite competent, isn't he?"

"He's more than that. The man is an investigating machine," Grace said. "I was beginning to wonder if there was anything left for us to do."

"That thought crossed my mind, too," I said. "But we've still got places to dig. Maybe we'll be able to turn something up on our own."

"Should we get started tomorrow when you close at eleven?" Grace asked.

"Can you take off that early from your job? We can postpone it until later, if that works out better for you."

Grace grinned at me. "My boss and her boss are both in London for a conference at corporate headquarters."

"I'm so sorry that you didn't get to make the trip yourself," Momma said.

"They're welcome to it. It's *way* above my pay grade, and while they might get to take fun trips now and then, the headaches they have in their jobs aren't worth the perks to me. I like things just fine the way they are."

"Then tomorrow at eleven it is," I said as I stifled a yawn. Between the wonderful dinner, that last slice of pie, and all that we'd done after I'd worked a full day at the donut shop, I was beat. I glanced at the clock on the wall and I saw that it was just after eight, which, sadly enough, was past my bedtime.

"I'll see you tomorrow," Grace said to me as she stood. Before she left, though, she leaned down and hugged my mother. "Thank you for a terrific dinner and dessert. You, my dear lady, are a magician in the kitchen."

"I'm glad that you enjoyed it. Do you have any requests for tomorrow night's meal?"

"Momma," I butted in. "We don't want you to feel as though you have to cook for us *every* night." Despite what I'd told Jake, I was a little reluctant to ask her to go to so much trouble on our account two nights in a row.

"Suzanne, I'm dying to try out a handful of new recipes, and the three of you are my perfect test subjects. You wouldn't deprive me of that, would you?"

"How could I?" I asked. "Any previews of what we might be having?"

"That depends on which mystery I pull off the shelf tonight."

After Grace left and I was upstairs drifting off to sleep, I realized that somewhere out there a murderer had struck less than twenty-four hours earlier. I wondered if we'd ever be able to find him, even with Jake's help.

Momma and I couldn't afford to have this case go unsolved.

There was too much at stake, including the memory of my dear, departed father. He might have been flawed, but he was still my dad, and I was going to do everything in my power to preserve the memories we had of him.

"Are you Suzanne?" a woman asked me the next morning as she came into the donut shop. She was in her late twenties, around twenty pounds overweight, and she had shiny black hair and the deepest, darkest eyes I'd ever seen in my life. We'd just been open a few minutes, and no one else had been in yet. When Emma had first arrived, she had peppered me with more questions about the murder, but since I had no real answers for her, we'd quickly fallen into our routine of early morning donut making. There was a definite rhythm to our movements, and I loved having her back by my side. At the moment I was up front working the counter alone, while she had her hands buried in soapy water in the kitchen sink, her iPod cranked up as usual when she worked alone.

"I'm Suzanne. Can I get you a donut?" I offered.

The woman looked surprised by my question, though I wasn't at all certain what she'd expected when she walked into my, you know, donut shop.

"Just coffee," she said. "Nothing fancy. Plain and black is fine by me."

"A woman after my own heart," I said. "My assistant loves to offer exotic blends to our customers, but I like mine old-fashioned."

I put the coffee down in front of her as she slid a ten on the counter toward me.

"We need to talk," she said.

"Well, since there's no pressing business at the moment, you've got my complete and undivided attention."

"My name is Heather Morningstar," she said.

"And you already know my name," I said as I offered her my hand.

She took it briefly, and then she said, "Angelica sent me."

As soon as she said that, things began to make a little more sense. "This is about the murder, isn't it?"

"It is. I understand that Morgan was blackmailing you, too."

"Too?" I asked, surprised by her statement. "Do you mean that he tried to get his hooks into you, as well?"

"There was no trying about it. He succeeded. You see, I couldn't afford to have my secret come out. It would have ruined everything. At least I thought so."

This was clearly going to take more than a minute. I said, "Would you excuse me for one second?"

After tapping Emma on the shoulder and nearly startling

her out of her tennis shoes, I said, "I need you to cover the
front for me."

"What?" she asked as the pulled out the earbuds.

"Cover for me, okay?"

"You got it, Boss," she said as she shut her iPod off.

I walked back out into the dining area to see what Heather
had to say, but it was empty.

Where had she gone?

Then I spotted her sitting at a table out front. It was
barely after seven, and the humidity had already started up in
full force, but if she could take it, then so could I.

"I'll be out front if you need me."

I grabbed a coffee for myself, and then I joined Heather
outside. "There you are. I thought for a second that you took
off on me."

"After what I just told you? That would be cruel." She
stared into her coffee cup for a few seconds, and then she
said, "Angelica told me that I could trust you, and that you
knew how to be discreet."

"That's sweet of her," I said, "but I won't keep anything
illegal from the police."

"Isn't paying off a blackmailer illegal in and of itself?"
Heather asked.

"That's not what I'm talking about; if you confess to
killing Morgan, I won't keep my mouth shut."

"I wouldn't expect you to. Will you keep my secret,
Suzanne?"

"If it's humanly possible, I will," I said. "But you should
know up front that doesn't include two people: my boyfriend,
Jake, and my best friend, Grace. He's an investigator for the
state police, but he's taking some time off to help me solve
this case, and she's my partner in the investigation. If you
don't want either one of them to know, too, then you'd better
not tell me."

Heather nodded. "Angelica already warned me, so I have
no problem with you sharing what I tell you with them, as
long as they don't blab, either."

"I can give you my word that they won't," I said. Jake, reticent by nature, would never violate a trust, and while Grace could be a little chatty on occasion, she'd keep quiet, too. I believed that enough to include her in the circle of those I trusted the most.

That left Momma, and I was about to say something about her when Heather said, "Angelica told me that you and your mother are close, and since she's directly involved in this, you have my permission to share it with her as well."

"Then we have a deal," I said. "Why was Morgan blackmailing you?"

Heather looked at me for a full ten seconds before she said, "Okay. Here goes. I'm engaged to the most wonderful man in the world, and we're getting married in three days."

"Congratulations," I said.

"Thank you. Anyway, Morgan came by my job five days ago and slid an envelope across my desk. We'd never met, and I was curious what it was about. When I opened the envelope and saw what was inside, I nearly fainted. I skipped the letter and looked at the photos first. They were all of me, taken years ago, a series that started with me fully clothed, and ended up with me just having a smile on my face, if you know what I mean." Her next words came out in a rush. "I'd foolishly agreed to let a boyfriend take them back when I was young and stupid and drunk."

"How did Morgan get his hands on them in the first place?"

"That's the first thing I asked him. It seems my ex had the pictures in prison with him, and Morgan won them in a poker game, of all things. That's not all that he won, but we'll get to that in a second."

"What did you do?"

"I was in shock, until my boss tapped on my door. I hurriedly shoved everything back into the envelope, but he must have seen something on my face. He asked me if I was okay, and I told him that I was fine, though he clearly didn't believe me. He kept glancing into my office, and I did my best to hustle Morgan out of there as fast as I could. I asked him what he wanted, and that's when he slid the wedding announcement I'd put in the newspaper the day before. He said that he needed ten grand for his silence, and if I paid him, I'd never see him, or the pictures, again."

"Did you have ten thousand dollars?" I asked.

"Not even close. There was only one way that I could get that kind of money, and it was from someone I'd *never* ask."

"Your fiancé?" I asked.

"Yes."

"So then, what did you do?"

"I tried to stall for time. We were going to meet yesterday, and when he didn't show up, I thought all was lost. Then I heard about the murder, and the flood of relief I felt was unbelievable, until I began to wonder where those photographs were now."

I could feel her pain, and though I'd never done anything quite that foolish myself, I hadn't always been the most levelheaded girl myself in the past. "So you came looking for me."

"Not at first, but Angelica's a friend of the family, kind of like an aunt to me, really. Not one of the stern ones, but a really cool one, you know?"

"I do," I said. "It just makes sense that you went to her with your problem."

"Not about the blackmail, but about Morgan Briar being murdered," she said. "There's just one thing. Cliff can't find out, and I mean *never*. He is ultraconservative, and this would ruin everything. If he knew that there were pictures of me out there like that, he couldn't handle it; I just know it."

"I understand," I said. "I wish I could help you, but I don't know what I can do."

"If you find my pictures when you're snooping around, I need them, and I mean desperately. I'll pay you as much as I can scrape up."

"I'm sorry, but I can't do that," I said.

Before I could continue, she interrupted, "Please,

Suzanne? I'll do anything."

"Heather, you didn't let me finish. If I find out where Morgan was hiding his blackmail stash, I'll see to it personally that you get your pictures back before anyone else gets a chance to see them. I hope you destroy them the second that you get them, but I won't take a dime from you. Do you understand?"

"Angelica told me that you had a good heart," she said. The relief was plain on her face, but I couldn't let her go on thinking that all was well and good now.

"I wouldn't celebrate quite yet, Heather. There's not much of a chance that I'll be able to find *anything* that he was hiding."

"I understand. It's just good to know that someone's out there trying to help me."

"Then we're good. Do you happen to know anyone else Morgan might have been blackmailing?"

"No, I'm sorry. He never mentioned anyone else to me."

I knew that it had been a long shot, but I'd taken it, anyway.

"Is there anything else you can tell me about him?"

"Not really," she said, and then she seemed to think about it for a few seconds before she spoke again. "He was so *casual* about it all, you know? I had a hunch that he'd blackmailed a few people before he got to me."

"How was he dressed when he came into your office?" I asked.

"He was wearing a suit, but it was clear that it was from the thrift store. The only thing odd was the rosebud he wore in his lapel. It didn't seem to match his demeanor, if that makes any sense. I'm sorry I couldn't be of more help."

"Don't worry. I'll do my best to help you bury your past."

Heather nodded, handed me a card, and then she said, "My cell number is on the back. Call me if there's *anything* that I can do." She paused, and then looked at me as she added, "Angelica says that I should tell Cliff what's going on before he marries me. What do you think?"

"I agree with her completely," I said. "Wouldn't you rather get this all behind you so that you can enjoy your wedding without worrying that the photos are going to show up at any second?"

"If I tell Cliff, I'm not sure there's even going to *be* a wedding," she said as she twisted a large diamond engagement ring on her finger.

"That says something right there, when you think about it. If your fiancé doesn't want you because of a past indiscretion, it might be better to know that up front. I know that I'd want to know."

"I'll think about it," she said. "Please find those photos, Suzanne."

"As I said, I'll do what I can," I said.

After Heather was gone, I grabbed my cell phone and called Jake. This was too big to keep until dinner tonight.

"I didn't wake you, did I?" I asked with a grin. Though he *never* awoke as early as I had to every day, I knew that usually he got up at six a.m., regardless of whether he was working on a case or not.

"I'm heading your way," he said. "As a matter of fact, I'm just across the street."

"Then hurry up. There's something I need to tell you."

"Look up," he said as he came from the Boxcar, waving.

I hung up my phone and met him halfway in the park. "Did you grab breakfast over there instead of coming by my place?"

"This was business," he said. "Sure, I had eggs and toast, but I had a meeting as well, and I thought it might be questionable having her meet me at Donut Hearts."

"Her?" I asked, putting a lot of emphasis into that single word.

"Martha Hickok," he said. "She's in her seventies now, but she must have been a real beauty back in her day."

"I'll have you know that women can still be beautiful when they hit the seven-decade mark," I said.

"Of course they can, but sometimes once the bloom is

faded, especially when the woman has sunbathed all of her life, it's a fast fall. Her skin looked more like aged leather, you know?"

"What was your meeting about?" I asked.

"It seems that Morgan was trying to blackmail her, too. She lives in Union Square, and she wanted to be certain that no one saw us talking, so I suggested Trish's place."

"That man was certainly busy, wasn't he?"

"Why, did you find another victim, too?"

I told him all about Heather, and the need to be discreet, which he was glad to promise.

"Wow, that's just crazy. He was really pushing his luck, wasn't he?" Jake asked.

"There's no doubt in my mind that's what got him killed," I agreed. "What I want to know is where his stash of blackmail information is right now?"

"I'll talk to Ellen and see if she'll let me look around," Jake said. "We're meeting in half an hour."

"Boy, you're squeezing them in pretty tightly, aren't you? How did Martha know to come to you?"

"Your mother gave her my number, as a matter of fact," Jake said, looking guilty about the confession.

"*My* mother?" I asked loudly. "Sure, that makes sense. Why wouldn't she tell her only child, someone she knew would be interested in the news?"

"Take it easy. All of this *just* happened. Martha called her to sympathize about the rumors going around about the two of you being involved in the mess, and she wanted to commiserate. Your mother knew that Martha responded much better to men than she did women, so she gave her my number, not yours. She was just doing what was best for our investigation, Suzanne. You shouldn't hold it against your mom."

It made sense the way Jake had explained it, but I still didn't have to love the idea.

"What did Martha have to say? Did she give you any details?" I knew that some folks had trouble sleeping as they

got older, which might have explained Martha's early
telephone call to my mother, but a great deal had been
happening already today, and it wasn't even eight o'clock yet.

"Funny, it's a lot like your story," Jake said. "She
claimed that Morgan had some direct evidence that Martha
had been less than discreet as a younger woman, a *much*
younger woman, I might add. When Morgan tried to
blackmail her with a photo sheet, Martha told him to have
them published in the newspaper if he could manage it. She
hadn't looked that good in decades, and she didn't care who
knew it."

"Did you say it was all printed on one sheet?" I asked.
Something Heather had said reminded me of Jake's
description.

"That's what she told me. Why?"

"I need to make a quick call first before I can say."

"Make it dance, Suzanne. I can't be late for my
appointment with Ellen," Jake said.

I dialed Heather's number. After she picked up, I asked,
"Were the photos of you single shots, or were they all printed
on one sheet?"

"They were all on one sheet. Why?" she asked.

"But the originals were Polaroids; that's what you told
me, right?"

"Yes. I told him that I wasn't about to pay for copies
when I saw that sheet. He promised me that if I paid up, I
could have them all, prints and originals both."

I didn't believe that Morgan would ever actually do that
for one second, but it was information I could use. "Was the
paper flat, like it came from a copier, or was it glossy, like it
originated in a lab?"

"It was glossy," she said. "You're on to something, aren't
you?"

"We'll see. Thanks for the information."

I turned to Jake, who'd been following my side of the
conversation. I said, "I've got a hunch that there's a photo lab
involved somewhere in this mess."

"Not necessarily. Suzanne, there are several ways of printing out photos on home computers that make them look as though they came straight from the lab."

"But Ellen told me that Morgan *hated* computers, and that he didn't know the first thing about using them. Plus, he prided himself on always knowing someone who could do whatever he needed. My guess is that he had private access to a photo lab. No developer at Photo World Picture Hut is going to make a proof sheet like the ones we've been talking about."

"So then I add that search to my list as well," he said.

"Hey, Greedy, leave something for the rest of us to do, okay?"

Jake looked a little like a small boy caught taking an extra cookie. "Sorry about that. Of course, you're right. You found the clue; you should be able to follow up on it. Besides, I'm so busy I don't know how I'm going to do everything on my schedule as it is." He bent forward, gave me a quick peck, and was on his way. "I'll talk to you later."

"I'm already looking forward to it," I said.

After he was gone, I thought about what I'd just learned. Morgan was a big-time blackmailer; there was no doubt about it, as evidenced by the victims who had come forward already. How many others were still out there that we didn't know about yet? As soon as I closed the donut shop, hunting for his photo shop connection was going to be a top priority, but I also wanted to know where he'd picked up that fresh rosebud. Was it from an innocent florist in the area, or could it have come from another victim? I didn't know the answer to that question, either, but I planned on finding out.

A little past ten, two men in workboots, dirty jeans, and faded T-shirts walked into the donut shop. "*Here's* where it is," one of them said, looking like a younger version of his companion. I was pretty sure that I was looking at a father and son.

"Where what is?" I asked, matching his smile.

"Where all the happiness in the world is," he said as he rubbed his hands together. "I don't know about you, Pop, but I could eat a dozen right here in the shop."

"Maybe when I was *your* age I could," he said, "but that was a long time ago."

"Then why don't you start with six and see how you do?"

"Do you honestly want eighteen donuts between the two of you to eat here?" I asked. I'd had some big donut eaters in the past, but never on that scale.

"Let's just start with two apiece and see how it goes," the elder said. "Is that okay with you, Henry?"

"Sure, but I can tell you right now that if they taste anything like they smell, we're going to be here awhile."

"What exactly can I get you?" I asked as I pulled out two trays.

"I'll take a couple of lemon-filled to start," the son said.

"Two plain cake donuts for me," his dad said.

"Come on; live a little, Pop," his son chided him.

He thought about it for a few seconds, and then said, "Okay, make it one plain cake, and one plain glazed donut, please."

"That's what you call living?" his son asked him.

"Ask me that same question when you get to be my age," the father said.

"Pop, I can't imagine *ever* being your age," he said with a bright smile.

"Trust me; it'll be here before you know it," the father said, and then he turned back to me. "Two coffees, too, please."

"Coming right up. If you'd like to grab a table, I'll bring everything over to you."

"The bar's just fine," he said.

As they took their seats, I grabbed their donuts and slid their requested orders in front of them. The coffees soon followed, and as I was about to walk away to clean up a little, the son told me, "You know, we could do a really nice counter out of mahogany if you'd like to dress the place up. It would look great."

I glanced down at the plain counter, and then I said, "Thanks, but this has worked out fine so far."

"Sure, it's okay," he said. "I'm just saying, you have a couple of world-class builders sitting right here at your counter, and if you promise us free donuts while we work, we'll quote you a good price, and we really would do an excellent job for you. Why don't you take a card, just in case."

Before I could reach for the offered card being slid across the counter, the father put an index finger on it, stopping its forward progress dead in its tracks.

"Apologize to the lady, Henry," the father said.

"Pop, if folks don't know we're available, how are we going to get new work down the road?"

"They seem to find us just fine as it is."

"Sorry," Henry said as he turned to me. "I get a little carried away sometimes."

"It's fine," I said. "Why don't you let me hold onto your card anyway?"

"You won't be sorry," Henry said, and I could tell that he was starting up with his sales pitch again when his father laid a hand on his son's shoulder.

"You'll have to forgive my son," the older man said with the hint of a laugh in his voice. "I just changed the business name from Jenkins Construction to Jenkins and Son, and I'm afraid that it's gone straight to his head. He's right, though. We do good work, and you could do a lot worse, *if* you ever need anything done around here."

"I'll remember that," I said as I put the card in a drawer up front with the others I received in the course of doing business. I didn't have a big remodeling budget—or any at all, actually—and I knew that I'd never in my lifetime be able to afford a new countertop, especially not one made of mahogany, of all things.

I'd be lucky to be able to afford a gallon of paint to cover the walls someday.

I did a little more cleaning, which was something that always seemed to be in order at the front of the donut shop counter whenever we were open, and as I started to top off the construction team's coffees, the older gentleman put his hand across the top of his cup. "Thanks, but we'd better not."

I asked, "Does that mean that you aren't ready to finish up that dozen donuts you were talking about earlier?"

"We might be able to do it, but we wouldn't get any work done today if we did," he said with a grin as he slid a ten across the counter. "The rest is for you. Have a nice day."

"You, too," I said. "Would you like those coffees to go?"

"No, we're fine," the father said. "Thank you, ma'am."

"It was my pleasure."

"We'll be back," the son said.

"I'm counting on it," I said. They would be a nice addition to my clientele. I loved how the father and son had interacted, and it made me wish that my father were still alive. We'd had that kind of relationship; at least I'd always thought so. Then I began to wonder if I really knew the man at all. This other life he'd lived in Union Square had all been news to me, and I tried to wrap my mind around it all, without much success. At least he'd had one good friend in his lowest time. I knew that Angelica was a valuable person to have on your side from firsthand experience, and somehow it comforted me knowing that she had been in his corner. If I were being honest with myself, I'd admit that there was a part of me that didn't *want* to keep digging into this case. My ignorance could be better than what I might find out if I kept looking into my father's earlier life, especially a part of it when Momma wasn't around.

But I really had no choice.

The only thing really going for Grace and me was the fact that Jake was working directly *with* us, and having him so actively involved in our investigation gave me confidence that ultimately we had a chance of solving Morgan Briar's murder.

Unfortunately, even though I didn't know it yet, that was

all about to change.

Chapter 9

"Suzanne, have you been listening to the news?" our mayor and my good friend, George Morris, asked urgently as he came rushing into the donut shop ten minutes before we were set to close. His face was pale, and he was nearly out of breath. From the expression on his face, something terrible must have just happened.

"No. Why? What's going on?" I asked, wondering what could rattle him so much.

"Somebody just tried to blow up the governor."

Chapter 10

"What!"

"Turn on your radio. It just happened," George said. I didn't have a television at the donut shop, and honestly, I'd never wanted one until that moment. I felt that Donut Hearts was a place to get away from the constantly squawking box, and the most I'd ever allowed was a small radio, usually tuned into a station that played classical music in the background, or one with hits from the past, and that depended on me even remembering to turn it on, which half the time, I forgot.

I turned it on now, though, searching for a station that broadcast the news, and sure enough, there was a bulletin on the air about the explosion.

"For those of you just joining us, let me repeat that an assassination attempt was just made on Governor Winston in Raleigh. Details are still sketchy, but it appears that a high-explosive device was detonated at 10:28 a.m. near the governor's automobile. If not for the governor's penchant to stop and shake hands with folks lined up to see him, he would have surely been killed in the explosion. Right now, there are reports that there were no fatalities at the scene; however, two members of the governor's security detail were injured in the explosion, as well as a high-ranking official with the state police. We'll keep you updated as the story develops."

Jake came bursting in as the announcer repeated the story, and he said, "Good, you've already heard the news. Suzanne, I've got to go. All vacation time has been canceled, as of right now. I don't know when I'll be back, but this is something that I've got to do. There will be a hundred different law enforcement agents working this case, but this is personal for me. My boss was filling in for me on the governor's detail when he got hurt. By all rights, that should have been *me* caught in that explosion, not him."

"Jake, it wasn't your fault," I said as I hugged him. Was it awful of me to feel relief that he *hadn't* been there? I didn't wish anything bad on his boss, but Jake was safe, and I'd be lying if I didn't admit that was more important to me.

"I should have been there," he repeated as he handed me a notebook. "Here's what I've got so far. You and Grace are going to have to do this without me. I'll call you as soon as I can, but don't wait up, okay?"

"Okay. Be careful."

He shook his head. "I'm not the one who needs to worry; whoever made that bomb is going to be in serious trouble if I'm the one who finds him."

After Jake was gone, I turned back to the radio, but it was just more of the same at that point. I looked at George as I told him, "Thanks for letting me know what happened. Can I get you a donut while you're here?"

"That's not such a bad idea," he said. "Suzanne, don't forget that I'm here if you need me."

"I could never forget you, George," I said.

"I mean that I can help you and Grace with your case," he replied. "Just because I'm mayor doesn't mean that I can't still snoop around with the best of them."

"I appreciate the offer more than I can tell you, but we both know there are some very good reasons why that's not a good idea."

"Suzanne, if I just did what was *sensible* all of the time, then I wouldn't be mayor, now would I?"

It was true that I was tempted by his offer to help, but I didn't want to put George in a position where it might jeopardize his job. But then again, looking at his earnest face, I couldn't just reject his offer outright, either. "I'll tell you what I'll do. If I get in a jam, you're the one I'll call, but not until then. Okay?"

"I suppose it will have to do," he said as he took the offered plain cake donut. "I'd better get back to the office. It's a sad day all around, isn't it?"

"I agree, but from where I'm looking, it could have been a whole lot worse," I said.

After George was gone, I walked back into the kitchen and found Emma up to her elbows in sudsy water. As usual, her iPod was blaring away, and after I tapped her on the shoulder, she grinned at me as she pulled off her earbuds. "Sorry, Boss, I must have gotten a little carried away with my music. I didn't even hear you walk back here." She must have seen the stern expression on my face, because she asked me, "What's wrong?"

"Somebody just tried to blow up the governor," I said, still not able to wrap my head around the fact. I knew that there had always been deranged madmen among us, but was it just me, or did they seem to be multiplying these days?

"Oh, no. Is he dead?"

"Fortunately, no one was killed in the explosion, but a few men were hurt. Jake's gone to help investigate it."

"Then I feel sorry for whoever did it. He'll find whoever's responsible," Emma said. "He's a good man."

"You don't have to tell me that."

Emma nodded, and then she asked, "Is that all?"

"I just thought you'd want to know."

"Thanks," Emma said as she put her earbuds back in and returned her attention to the dishes. Had she grown so accustomed to the insanity in the world that it didn't faze her anymore? Different generations, I guess, or perhaps it was the knowledge that it might easily have been Jake who'd been injured that had brought it closer to home to me. I hoped that my boyfriend had a hand in finding the bomber if they managed to hunt him down, but I couldn't spend too much time worrying about that right now. I was heading up my own investigation again, with Grace by my side, and I had plenty to worry about all on my own. I glanced through Jake's notebook, and I saw that in his fine hand, he'd laid out not only what he'd done so far, but his plans for the future. It was an excellent glimpse into his methodically trained thought process, and there was no doubt in my mind that he was good at what he did. It seemed to be in stark contrast to the way that Grace and I dug into our cases, mostly just making it up as we went along. By the time Emma and I were ready to close Donut Hearts for the day, I'd read through his notes three times. There were several leads worth following up on, but for the most part, I was going to keep digging until something valuable turned up.

"I don't understand people these days," Grace said as she walked into the donut shop after I let her in ten minutes later. Emma was already gone, and I was just finishing up with my deposit for the day. I could have easily closed earlier, since no one had come into the shop after I'd heard the news about the governor. I suppose they were all at home or at work, glued to their television sets. "Can you believe this is really happening?"

"I know. It's still sinking in. Have there been any new developments?"

"Just rampant rumors and speculation all over the airwaves," she said. "I'll bet Jake is chomping at the bit to get involved."

"They've already called him in," I said. "I'm afraid that it's just going to be the two of us from here on out."

Grace nodded. "I kind of figured that it might be. Butch and Sundance, alone again."

"I'd rather think that we were the good guys, not a pair of outlaws," I said with the hint of a grin. No matter how grim the situation, I knew that I could always count on Grace to lighten the mood.

"Okay, have it your way. What's on tap for this afternoon?"

"As soon as we drop my deposit off at the bank, we need to go to Union Square."

"Who do we talk to first?"

"I want to go to Garrett's Camera Shop," I said. I'd

looked up specialty stores that sold photographic equipment and offered developing services in the area, and Garrett's was by far the closest to where Morgan had been staying with his sister. If anyone could give me a lead about who might have reproduced those shots for Morgan, it would be them. I knew that the odds weren't in my favor, but it was a lead that needed to be followed up on, and whether it was law enforcement trying to solve the case or just Grace and me, some of the same steps still had to be followed.

"Garrett's it is," she said.

The till balanced to the penny, always a happy event, and after we dropped off the deposit, we drove to Union Square, talking about what would drive someone to do such a crazy thing to the governor. By the time we pulled up in front of Garrett's in my Jeep, we hadn't come any closer to finding an answer, and I realized that sometimes, there *was* no answer. It was a hard pill to swallow, knowing that there were times when the world just didn't make sense. Momma liked to say that was why she enjoyed her cozy mysteries; the bad guy always got his due in the end.

It was a real shame that life wasn't like that nearly enough.

"Excuse me, can you help us?" I asked the short, thin man behind the counter of the camera shop. He had sharp brown eyes and a fading hairline that told me that he'd be bald soon enough. The shop was full of camera equipment for sale, as well as brightly colored posters depicting scenes from waterfalls, picnics, and several other pleasing scenarios.

"Of course. I'd be delighted to offer any assistance that I can. What kind of camera would you like? I've just gotten a new line of SLRs that are absolutely fantastic. They are on sale this week, with a nice additional lens and case included free." I saw from his nametag that his name was Jackson Garrett; it appeared that the owner himself was waiting on us.

"I should have explained myself. We're not here looking for a camera," I said, and the man visibly deflated a little.

These were tough times for our part of North Carolina, just as they were in the rest of the country, and quite a few small business owners I knew were hanging on for dear life. At least folks were willing and able to still treat themselves to donuts every now and then. It was quite a smaller financial commitment than the wares he was offering, and I was very glad of it.

"Film, perhaps?" he asked.

"No, sorry. Actually, we're here looking for someone who develops film on the side."

"I can handle that for you," he said as he retrieved an empty envelope from a stack on the counter.

"These are special," I said.

"I'm sorry, but I don't do that sort of thing," he said, refusing to make eye contact with either one of us now.

I supposed that I had that coming. "You don't understand. It's not like that."

"Actually, it kind of is," Grace said.

"You're not helping," I told her, and then I turned back to the owner. "Where could we get a series of photographs printed on a single sheet of paper?"

"Any good color inkjet printer could do it," he said.

"This was on photographic paper," I replied. "I'm not explaining myself very well, am I?"

Mr. Garrett reached over to a nearby section and selected a thin packet with the dimensions of a regular sheet of paper. "This is what you're looking for."

I was about to protest when I looked at the heading on the package and read that the paper was indeed photographic paper, fit for any inkjet printer.

Jake was right. Anyone could do it. But they had to be able to use a computer, and we knew that Morgan hadn't had even rudimentary skills in that area.

I didn't know much about computers or printers, but Grace clearly had a thought. "Do the images have to be scanned into the computer first, or can they just be copied?"

"With the right machine, they can be copied right onto the

paper," he answered. "There's so much folks can do for themselves these days, and when you add that to online shopping, a lot of my old customers don't even bother coming in here at all."

I was about to commiserate when Grace grabbed my arm. "Let's go, Suzanne."

I turned to Mr. Garrett and said, "Thank you for your time."

"You're welcome to it. It's mostly all I have these days," he said.

After we were out on the sidewalk in front of the photography shop, I asked Grace, "Why were you so abrupt in there?"

"Suzanne Hart, I know you. We were going to be there for half an hour talking about the plight of small business owners, and we can't afford to do that; we have a case to solve."

I started to protest, and then I realized that Grace most likely was right. I *did* tend to empathize a little too much at times. I could feel the man's pain, but there was nothing I could do about it. If I ever did buy a fancy camera, though, I'd try to go back there to shop for it, but I knew that most likely wasn't going to happen. It still saddened me about how many businesses were feeling the pinch of a lingering bad economy.

"I've never really done much printing myself," I told Grace once we were back in her car. "I didn't know that there were so many options. Heck, I don't even have a computer at the donut shop. If I need to get online, I just use Momma's setup at home."

"I use one all of the time for work," Grace said, "but I've never needed to copy photographs before. So, that's another dead end."

"I'd say so. Clearly Morgan Briar found *someone* to help him with those photographs, but I have no idea how we find him."

"Then what's next on our list?"

"It's on to the florist," I said. "Hopefully, we'll have better luck there."

"We're here about a tight red rosebud," I told the woman behind the floral counter at Budding Hope Flowers. For some reason, she looked familiar to me, but I couldn't place her right away. "Do you sell many boutonnières these days?" "Not often, but we get customers requesting them occasionally." She was in her late twenties, and had flaming red hair that was pulled back into a ponytail. There was a sparkle in her eyes, and she looked like a diehard romantic, but then again, she'd almost have to be to own a flower shop, wouldn't she? To add a little icing to the cake, her nametag said Rose, of all things.

"Is that really your name?" I asked her with a smile. "Were you doomed to this life from the start?"

"I'm Rose, but I don't consider it a curse. My parents were all set to name me Evelyn, but the second they saw my red hair, they changed it to Rose. Besides, I find it a fortunate coincidence. I love this place."

Rose clearly displayed the same love of her flower shop that I did with my donut place, and I felt a little bit of the kindred spirit in her. "The question about the rosebud is important, so if you can help us, we'd greatly appreciate it."

"Why are you asking?" she asked as she studied Grace and me carefully.

"We saw a man wearing one the other day, and it made us curious. He was dressed in a black suit, his build was kind of on the smallish side, and he obviously loved the flower he was wearing."

I saw Rose cringe for just a second as I described Morgan Briar, and I knew that we'd hit pay dirt. "Did you sell one of your flowers to him?"

"I sell a great many blooms throughout the course of a day," she said. "I have no idea if your friend got it from here, or somewhere else. Why do you really want to know? Would you like one for the man in your life? We can take

care of that, or you can look around for something else."
Rose started to turn her back to us, but I wasn't about to
let her brush us off that easily. "Actually, it's the man himself
that we want to talk to you about. Just how well did you
know Morgan Briar?"

Rose hesitated just a second too long for her answer to be
legitimate, as though she had weighed her options before
deciding exactly how to reply. "I don't have a clue who
you're talking about. Sorry. If you aren't interested in
buying anything, feel free to look around. I need to do a little
inventory on our accessories."

Rose looked around the shop, picked up a clipboard, and
then she started writing on the top sheet on it. Though I
couldn't see the paper that she was working on, I had a hunch
that it could have just as easily been a lunch menu from the
diner across town.

"Rose, it's important that we talk to you," Grace said to
the florist as she moved closer. I was perfectly happy to let
my friend take the lead from here on out, if she could make
better progress than I'd been able to so far. "You're not alone
in this. He was blackmailing my friend, too," Grace added
softly. I wasn't at all certain that it was the right thing to say,
but then again, her instincts had advanced our investigations
in the past enough to earn her a little slack questioning this
woman.

"I'm sorry for your trouble, but I can't help you," Rose
said, but I could see from her expression that something was
deeply troubling her.

She went back to her list, though, and it appeared that this
was going to be another dead end.

Then Antonia DeAngelis walked in.

"Suzanne, Grace, what are you two doing here? I doubt
that you're shopping for flowers this far from home."

"You know us," I said. "We're digging into that murder
we told your mother about."

Rose pretended to ignore us, but it was clear that she was
hanging on every word.

Antonia nodded. "If there's anything we can do to help, all you have to do is ask. I don't have to tell you that my mother is your biggest fan." She turned to Rose and said, "We need to change the next floral delivery to add more roses to the settings. It's not too late to make a change, is it?"

"Of course not. Tell your mother that I'll personally take care of it myself."

"Excellent," Antonia said, and then she smiled at us and added, "I just *love* delivering good news."

As Antonia left, she waved to us, and then she walked back toward Napoli's.

"Do you two really know Angelica?" Rose asked us in a soft voice ten seconds later.

"We do. If you'd like to call her to check, it wouldn't hurt my feelings a bit," I said.

"There's no need to do that. Antonia's word is good enough for me." Rose took a deep breath, and then she let it out slowly. "To answer your earlier question, I knew him, and yes, the little weasel got that flower from me. I didn't kill him, but I'd love to present a bouquet to whoever did."

"I take it then that you were a victim as well," I said gently.

"Oh, yes. He found out something about my aunt, and he used it to blackmail me. If word got out about what she'd done, it would kill her. Now, I keep waiting for someone to find the evidence that Morgan was using against her."

"We're searching for his stash ourselves," Grace said. "If we find anything that will help you out, we'll hand it over if we can."

"You would do that for me, a stranger?" she asked.

"You're not a stranger," I said. "We just haven't met before today, but if you're friends with the DeAngelis family, then you're our friends as well."

A hint of relief entered her eyes, if only briefly. "I'll tell you what I can, but it's not much."

"At this point, we'll take whatever we can get," Grace said.

"I know that ever since he got out of prison, Morgan has been drinking with a guy named Larry Landers. Larry never has been all that great a guy, but whenever Morgan was around, he got a whole lot worse. He might know what Morgan was up to that got him killed."

Were we finally getting a real lead? It was almost too good to be true. "Thanks so much for your help," I said.

"There's one more thing," Rose said before we got out the door. "I don't know if it matters, but I saw Morgan coming out of the bus station a few days before he was murdered. He was alone, and he had a brown paper bag like they use at the grocery store tucked under his arm. It was empty, and I could swear that he was smiling. It really gave me the creeps."

"That's great," I said as I handed her one of my business cards from the donut shop. One of my customers had made them the year before as a Christmas present, and I kept some in my wallet, just in case. "If you think of anything else, don't hesitate to give me a call at the donut shop."

"I've been there before," she said. "My downfall is your Lemon Delight donut. How do you make that glaze so perfectly every time?"

So that's where I'd seen her. She'd been in my shop. I couldn't be too hard on myself for not realizing it at first. I had quite a few customers that came by so infrequently that I'd never be able to consider them regulars. "I'd love to say that it was from years of hard work and experimentation, but it was actually just a happy coincidence one day." I'd accidentally dusted a run of lemon-glazed donuts with powdered sugar, and then I'd put them too close to the heat. The glaze and the sugar had combined in a magic way that gave everything a bigger pop, and it was now one of my best sellers. "I'll bring you some the next time I'm in Union Square."

"Just one," she said. "I tend to get a little carried away with your donuts. That's why I can't get them very often."

"Okay, one it is. We'll be in touch, Rose."

"I really hope that you find Morgan's stash of proof

before someone else discovers it and decides to use it, too," Rose said.

"So do we," Grace replied.

Chapter 11

Out on the sidewalk, Grace looked around for a few seconds, and then she asked me, "Should we go off in search of the mysterious Larry Landers now?"

"First, we need to go to the bus station," I said. "I've got a hunch something's up with what Rose just told us."

"Lead on, then."

We walked into the station and saw a half dozen rows of benches, a ticket window with a grumpy old man sitting behind it, and a double row of lockers, most of them with orange-handled keys still in their locks. "I'm willing to bet good money that Morgan's blackmail info is in one of these lockers," I said.

"I agree, but which one?" she asked as she surveyed them. "The numbers go up to two hundred, and at least twenty of them don't have keys in them. We can't break into *all* of them."

I laughed. "Grace, we aren't going to break into *any* of them, but if we run across a key somewhere that matches the ones they use here, we know where to come." I stepped forward, tried to pull out a key from one of the open lockers, but it wouldn't budge.

Grace said, "Allow me," as she pulled three quarters out of her purse. Once they were accepted, the key came out easily enough. "Do *we* need a locker for something?" she asked me as she handed me the key.

"No, but this might come in handy before this is all over," I said as I tucked it into my blue jeans.

"Now do we go looking for Larry?" Grace asked me.

"I'm game if you are," I said. "Where should we start looking?"

"You heard Rose. He and Morgan were big drinking

buddies. I say we find the nearest bar and see if we have any luck. If he's not there, I'm willing to wager that someone there will know where we can find him."

As we got out of my Jeep at the bar at the edge of town, Grace said, "Let me handle this, Suzanne."

"Hey, I've *been* in a bar before; maybe more than you have," I said. That probably wasn't true, though, for several reasons. It took a real occasion for me to drink anything even *remotely* alcoholic, and besides, my hours didn't exactly make drinking a viable option, not when I had to go to bed so early every night in order to run the donut shop. I usually considered a glass of wine a cause to celebrate, so maybe Grace should lead the way.

She just laughed at my statement. "Between some optimistic dates trying to get me liquored up, and a few obnoxious buyers trying to purchase more than I had for sale, I highly doubt that."

"Okay, your point is conceded," I said. "You lead."

As we walked into the bar, it took some time for my vision to get accustomed to the lower level of light inside. There was an old jukebox playing quietly in one corner, and a long bar spanned the entire length of the back with its own set of stools; tables and booths were scattered everywhere else around the room. The air conditioning was cranked up to its full capacity, and the shock of feeling the cold air after being outside in the heat was jarring at first. As my vision grew more accustomed to the dark, I noticed that there were half a dozen men and one woman already drinking, most of them in somber solitude.

Grace started to approach the bartender as we both heard one man on the end say, "Larry, you always were a blowhard. You haven't been on a date with a woman in a year, and everybody in this room knows it."

Grace changed her course without missing a step and headed straight for the man in question. As she approached him, she said teasingly, "Larry, there you are. I thought you stood me up again."

I hung back and watched my friend lie with such poise and ease.

To Larry's credit, he played right along. "You know that I wouldn't do that to you, baby. I just lost all track of time." He tried to kiss her, but Grace deftly turned her cheek as he moved forward.

"Now come on," she said as she tugged at his arm. "We're going to be late for the movie, and you *know* how I hate that." Grace waved to the man Larry had been talking to, and then I saw her wink at him. He couldn't have been more surprised if she'd handed him a hundred dollar bill and asked him to dance.

I moved outside first, amazed by the difference in the temperature from conditioned to raw air.

Larry started laughing the second the door to the bar closed behind us. "Lady, I have no idea who you are, but I owe you a drink, any place, any time. Did you see Steve's face? I thought he was going to have a coronary."

"I need something more than a drink in exchange for my little performance in there, Larry. Tell me what you know about Morgan Briar, and his dirty little secret."

Larry's expression went from sheer joy to cold suspicion in less than a second. "Sorry, but I don't know what you're talking about."

"Larry," Grace said gently. "Do you really want me to go back in there and tell Steve the truth?"

He was clearly horrified by the mere thought of it. "You wouldn't do that to me, would you? Come on, give a guy a break."

"It's your choice," Grace said, and I didn't doubt for one second that she meant every word of it.

Larry must have understood it as well, because his shoulders suddenly slumped as he said, "Okay. You win. I'll tell you whatever you need to know. Only can we get out of this blasted heat? I'm about to melt out here."

"Do you really want to risk going back into the bar?"

Grace asked.

"No way. There's a laundromat over there, though. It'll do."

It was an odd place to hear his confession, but I had to agree with him. If it got us out of the heat, it was good enough for me. We followed Larry into Suds Suds Suds, and there was a corner where we could have a conversation without any of the other three patrons listening in.

"Okay, no one's within earshot, and we're out of the heat," I said to Larry. "Now tell us what you know about Morgan's dirty little side business."

Larry sighed heavily, and then ran a hand through his greasy hair before he spoke. "Morgan and I were friends long before he went to jail, and we took right back up once he got out. That man didn't deserve what he got, not out in the free world, and not when he was behind bars."

I wasn't about to debate the man's fate with Larry. "Tell us exactly what he's been up to since he got out of prison," I asked.

"Why do *you* want to know?" Larry asked. It was clear that he was more than a little suspicious of our motives.

"The truth? We're trying to find his killer," Grace said.

"I don't understand why you would, when his own sister doesn't care about what happened to him," he said as a hint of irritation frosted his words. "Why *do* you?"

"You don't need to know the exact details," I said. "Let's just say that we're helping out a friend."

Larry seemed to take that in, and then he said, "Then it's not out of any particular love of my dead friend. Is that what you're saying?"

He had a legitimate point, but I couldn't let that stop me. "Larry, does it really matter *why* my friend and I are looking for Morgan's killer? Aren't you glad that at least *someone's* digging into this? How much effort do you think that the police are going to put into finding out what happened to a guy like Morgan? If he's going to get any justice at all, it's most likely going to be up to us."

I wasn't at all certain how much of that I honestly believed myself, but there was enough truth in it to satisfy Larry. "Okay, I'll tell you what I know, but it's not much. Morgan never really shared too much of anything with anybody."

"You still knew him better than anybody else did," Grace said soothingly.

"Maybe, maybe not."

"Who knew him better than you?" Grace asked. "His sister?"

"Ellen? No way. She was always on his back about finding a job and a getting his own place to live. Morgan was going to leave as soon as he got some money he had coming to him, and that's a fact."

"Where was he getting it?" I asked.

Larry just shrugged. "He wouldn't tell me, but it sounded like a pretty decent amount."

I knew where that money was supposed to be coming from, even if Larry was pretending not to know himself. It was time to stop tap dancing around the truth. "How many people was he blackmailing?" I asked softly.

Larry was *not* a consummate poker player. He pursed his lips for a moment, frowned, and then he studied his hands before he spoke. "I don't know what you're talking about."

"Come on, Larry. How is this going to hurt Morgan now? It's not like he can be arrested because of anything he might have done while he was alive."

Grace spoke up, adding, "Unless you were in on it, too, there's *no* reason that you shouldn't tell us now."

"How do I know that you won't go to the cops?" Larry asked, and then added a bit too late, "Not that I know anything."

"You have our word on it," I said. "If you weren't involved in his blackmailing attempts, you don't have anything to fear from the two of us."

Grace looked at me quizzically and asked, "Should you really be promising him something like that?"

"I meant what I said," I answered. "It's the only way Larry's going to tell us anything, and information is what counts right now." I turned back to Larry and said, "Go on. We're listening, and it won't go any further than this laundromat."

He thought about it for a full minute before he finally replied. "If anybody finds out that I told you about this, it could be very bad for me; do you understand?"

"We promise," I said, and Grace nodded as well, albeit reluctantly. "We do," she added.

"Okay. I'm going to trust you both. I just hope that it doesn't come back and bite me later. Morgan got drunk one night and I had to walk him home, but not right away, if you know what I mean. His sister doesn't drink, not really, and she didn't want him doing it, either. I had to sober him up a little. We walked for half an hour before he was in any shape to go into the house, and while we were strolling through the neighborhood, he started talking about his grand plans."

"Did you get any names out of him?" I asked.

"Let's see. There was a woman and her daughter in April Springs, and he also told me about a florist named Rose."

"Who else?"

Larry shook his head as he frowned. Evidently this was tougher for him than he thought it would be. "There was a woman named Heather, too."

"Is there *anyone* else that you can think of?" I asked. "Think, Larry." I had to know how big the pool of victims really was, because that was our list of suspects in the man's murder.

"Just one more," Larry said. "But I think I might have said too much already."

"You might as well tell us everything," I said. "You'll feel better if you get it all off your chest, I promise."

"Maybe I will. Okay, he also was trying to put the touch on another woman in April Springs."

Who else had Morgan gone after? I thought about all of my friends and acquaintances, but I couldn't imagine any of them having anything they had to hide.

"Go on. You've got our attention," Grace said. "Tell us her name."

"It's a woman named Polly North. She's been dating the mayor in April Springs, even though he's her boss."

I laughed out loud at the supposed revelation. "It's no secret, Larry. Everyone knows they've been seeing each other on the sly." I felt relieved knowing how far off-base Morgan had been with at least part of his blackmail scheme. The man must have been really desperate.

"That wasn't the secret, according to Morgan," Larry said.

My laughter died in my throat, and I believe that I must have choked a little on it as it did.

"What could she have possibly been blackmailed about?" Grace asked.

"It was her husband," Larry admitted. "Morgan claimed to have evidence that the man had a little help from his wife there in the end. He wasn't sure that it had been all that appreciated, or even done with his knowledge, if you know what I mean."

"Hang on a second," I said, forgetting to keep my voice low. "Are you telling me that you're accusing Polly North of killing her husband, a man everyone knows that she loved? Even if she wanted to, Polly barely weighs ninety pounds. It's ludicrous to even think that."

"So you know her, then," Larry said.

"Our paths may have crossed a time or two in the past," I said. Larry still didn't realize that I was the daughter being blackmailed, and if I had my way, he would *never* know.

"*I'm* not accusing her of anything," Larry said. "All I'm telling you is what Morgan told me. I don't even know the woman."

"For a man who supposedly had a lot of evidence," I said, "not a single bit has shown up so far. If you want to know the truth, I'm starting to wonder if he was just making it all up."

"You don't know about the key, do you?" Larry asked softly.

I looked at Grace, who stared back at me. How should we answer this one?

Before either one of us could say a word, though, Larry said, "Don't bother trying to deny that you knew about the key. I could see it by the way you just looked at each other. You both know."

"Where is the key, Larry?" I asked, doing my best to keep my voice level. Whatever was in that locker might be able to answer questions about my father that I never would have believed I'd be asking. It also could hold the fates of several other women I'd recently met.

"I don't *know*," Larry said, the disappointment in his voice clear to anyone within earshot. "I don't even know where to start looking for it. Do you?"

"Think about it, Larry. If we knew where the key was, why would we need to hunt you down?" Grace asked. "That wouldn't make much sense, now, would it?"

"Then it's lost forever," Larry said.

"Just because we haven't found it doesn't mean that we won't," I said.

"Well, I'm giving up," he answered. "It's just not worth it to me. I'm not going to jail over something that I didn't do."

"That sounds like a good plan," I said. "My friend and I are going to find that key, and when we do, we're going to turn it over to the police. Do you have any suggestions where we might look?"

He shook his head. "I don't have a clue; I've looked everywhere that I could think of. Sorry, but you're on your own. Can I go now? I've told you everything I know."

Grace glanced at me, shrugged, and I said, "Go, and thanks for your help. If I were you, I wouldn't mention this conversation to anyone else."

"As far as I'm concerned, it never happened," he said.

Larry started to walk out of the laundromat, and I spoke loudly enough so that everyone there could hear me. "Larry, if you *do* happen to find that key and try to use anything you find, you're going to regret the day you were ever born. Do you understand what I'm telling you?"

"I'm not worried about the two of you," Larry said, trying to brush off my threat.

I wasn't about to let him, though. "You should be. We've got friends everywhere, on both sides of the law. All it would take would be one word, and you'll regret the day you ever crossed us."

He studied Grace and me for a second with a mixture of anger and fear on his face, and then Larry slunk out of there before I could say another word.

Grace waited until we could see him walking back into the bar when she turned to me and spoke. "Wow, you had *me* going there with that last bit, and I've known you my entire life. That was some bluff."

"What makes you think I was bluffing?" I asked, keeping my expression as steady as I could.

"Hey, Suzanne, now you're scaring *me* a little."

"Don't worry; you're not the one who should be afraid. I just hope that Larry took me seriously there at the end."

"How could he not? So, what should we do now?"

I glanced at my watch. "If we hurry, we might be able to catch Polly before she leaves her office for the day."

"What are we going to tell George?" Grace asked.

"Whatever we need to. This isn't the time to tiptoe around our suspects. We need to ask Polly for the truth."

"George isn't going to like that very much," Grace said.

"I'm not too fond of the prospect myself, but what else can we do?"

We made it back to town, found a parking spot for the Jeep in front of the municipal building, and Grace and I bolted up the steps two at a time to try to catch Polly.

She was already gone, though.

There was a note on her door addressed to George, though.

It said,

Boss,

Meet me at the Boxcar. I have that report you've been looking for.
Polly.

Grace looked at me after we both read it. "It appears that we're going to be doing this with an audience."

"I don't think so," I said, shaking my head. "There's no way that we're going to ask the questions we need to ask Polly in front of everyone else at the diner."

"Well, we can't exactly hang around, and then ambush her when she leaves the Grill," Grace said.

"No, that would be just as bad. I need to call her and see if she'll meet us somewhere else right now."

"I'm glad that you're doing it instead of me," she said. "That's why you're the lead investigator, right?"

"I suppose so," I said as I dug out my phone and searched in its database for Polly's number. It was a call that I definitely didn't want to make, but the alternatives were even worse. At least I wouldn't have to find a way not to tip George off about the real reason I wanted to question his secretary and current girlfriend.

It wasn't much, but I'd take it.

Chapter 12

"Polly, I'm so sorry that I'm interrupting your dinner, but Grace and I need to talk to you, and it might be in your best interest if George doesn't know anything about it." I'd rehearsed that line a few times, trying to get as much information into it as I could. It had come out as though it had been stoppered in a bottle, spilling out over the phone in one long rush.

"I see," she said calmly. "And you're certain that it needs to be now?"

"The sooner, the better," I said. "We can meet you anywhere you'd like. Just make up an excuse for George, and let us know where you want to talk. We wouldn't ask if it weren't important."

"Yes, I understand. I'll be home shortly, and thank you for calling."

She hung up on me, and Grace asked, "What did she say?"

"We're supposed to meet her at her house soon," I said. "The woman didn't miss a beat when she heard what I had to say. She could have been a spy."

"Who knows? Maybe she was," Grace said.

"In another life, right? I wonder if we should just go over to her place and wait for her there?"

Grace shook her head. "Let's hang around here and see if George takes her home, or if they split up."

"He'll know my Jeep," I said. We'd been friends for too long for him *not* to know what I was up to, even if he *hadn't* been a cop before he retired.

"Then we'll park it at the Donut Shop and he'll just figure that you left it there. Come on, we need to move, Suzanne. I don't know how much time we have."

I backed my Jeep into a spot that allowed us a clear view of the Boxcar, and we sat chatting until we saw George and

Polly driving toward us in separate cars.

"Duck," I said as I grabbed Grace's shoulder.

"Beat you to it," she said as she slid silently down in her seat.

Once they got out onto Springs Drive, George followed Polly out of the parking lot, and I waited a full thirty seconds before I pulled out myself.

"If you don't hurry, you're going to lose them," Grace said urgently.

"First off, we already know where they're going, and second, if I left any earlier, George would have surely spotted us. Take it easy."

We crept along until we got to Polly's place, and I held my breath as I searched the driveway for George's car, but thankfully, it wasn't there.

We'd just parked and climbed out of the Jeep when Polly came walking quickly toward us. "Okay, ladies, I hate subterfuge, and I dislike lying to my employer and friend even more. You need to tell me what this is all about right now."

"It concerns your late husband," I said.

Polly seemed to fade just a little when she heard that, and with a weary sigh, she turned to her front porch and said, "You might as well come inside."

We did as she suggested, and after we were seated in her neat and tidy living room, Polly stared hard at me and asked, "What about him?"

"Somebody tried to blackmail you about him in the past few days, didn't they?"

Polly looked at me as though I had just sprouted three heads. "How could you possibly know that?"

"He's tried to extort money from us, too," I said. "What did *you* tell him to do?"

"I said that he could go howl at the moon or take out an ad in the paper if he wanted to, but I wasn't paying him a cent. How did you hear about it? I didn't tell *anyone*, not even George."

I had no trouble believing that Polly would take such a stand. The woman was many things, but a coward was not one of them.

There was a question that I had to ask, one that seemed to stick in my throat before I could even get it out. "Someone told us today that you might have killed your late husband. Is there any truth to it?" I asked, trying my best not to cry as I asked her the hardest question I'd had to ask anyone in recent memory.

She hesitated for nearly a minute before answering, and then Polly finally said, "From one point of view, I suppose I did."

"What point of view is that?" Grace asked. I wasn't the only one holding my breath waiting for her answer, but we weren't going to get it, at least not right away.

"You both remember my late husband, don't you?"

"Vaguely," I said, and Grace nodded as well. "He always played Santa at the library Christmas party, right?"

Polly's stern look softened for a moment. "He did indeed, up until the very end. Van weighed two hundred and twenty pounds at one point, and I kept warning him that if he didn't lose weight, he wasn't going to be around long enough to enjoy our retirement. At first I thought he was listening to me, because the weight suddenly started dropping off like crazy. I accused him of secretly exercising behind my back, but he denied it. He did lose some of his appetite, but it couldn't account for the weight he was losing. I finally talked him into going to a doctor to get checked out, but it turned out that we were too late. Cancer was eating away at him, and I was too blind to see it."

I reached out and patted her hand. "How could you have known? You can't beat yourself up about something like that."

"I appreciate the sentiment, but I still have a difficult time believing it, even if the doctors later confirmed that it was true," Polly said as a few tears trickled down her cheeks. If she noticed them at all, she didn't react to them. "In two

months, I hardly recognized him. We were told that the
cancer was spreading fast, and that it wouldn't be long, but
none of the specialists took my husband's spirit into
consideration. The hospice nearly gave up on him, but one
nurse stayed by his side during the day while I worked, and I
took the night shift here alone. Long past the date they'd
given him, he was still here in his hospital bed, each day
worst than the last. I couldn't *stand* seeing him in such pain."

Polly hesitated, but I kept my mouth shut. I wanted her to
be able to tell this at her own pace, and I could see that Grace
was willing to wait her out as well. After a few moments of
silence, Polly continued. "I'm ashamed to admit it, but one
night, in his darkest hour, I urged him to just let go, and I told
him that I'd see him on the other side. He finally agreed that
he just couldn't take it anymore, and he begged me to help
him. I put together a mixture of all of his drugs; ones we
were told would be a deadly combination. I dissolved
everything in a glass of water, added a touch of sugar to make
it a little sweeter going down, and I walked into that bedroom
ready to do what he'd asked me to.

"When I got there, he was already gone."

Now her crying came in earnest, this time in a steady
flow, as though she'd wanted to tell that particular story for a
long time.

After a full minute, Polly got her composure back, and she
finally said, "If I'd stayed with him, he wouldn't have had to
die alone. I should never have said a word. Because of my
selfishness, he had to die alone, and I can never forgive
myself for that."

"Polly," I said as I put an arm around her shoulder, "You
didn't *give* him the drugs."

"No, but according to my pastor, the thought is as bad as
the deed, and I was surely willing to help him cross over. If
he'd been alive when I walked into that bedroom, I would
have done it, ten times out of ten. So you see, in a way, I
really did kill him."

Grace spoke softly. "How can you be certain that you

would have gone through with it, though? You could have changed your mind at the last second, and so could he."

"Not my dear, sweet, stubborn husband. His mind was made up," Polly said, refusing to be let off the hook.

"You said it yourself, though," I chimed in. "Things can change in an instant. Are you telling us right now that if he'd told you that he'd changed his mind and that he wanted to live, that you wouldn't have flushed those drugs down the toilet?"

"No, I can't say that," she admitted.

"There's something else you aren't considering," I added. "Maybe he was just tired of fighting, and he decided to just let go. It's not unheard of, you know."

"There are too many ifs and theories, though," Polly said. "I can't ever know what *might* have happened, can I?"

"That's the whole point. None of us can. Polly, if it were me in that bed, I'd hope that *someone* would have the courage to help me."

"As much as I hate the thought of it, I'd do it for you," Grace said.

"I'd do it for you, too," I said, happy that I had someone who cared more about me than the consequences her actions might bring. I was suddenly aware of the fact that all three of us were crying now.

"The thing is, who knew what you'd done?" I asked as I wiped away my tears. "Did you tell anyone?"

"Not then, but later, a police officer came by the house to interview me," Polly said.

"It wasn't George, was it?" I asked her, hoping that they hadn't met through such a cruel set of circumstances.

"No, as a matter of fact, it was a woman officer on loan from the Union Square Police Department. I told her everything, and she *promised* me that no one could arrest me for what had happened. She was very reassuring, in her own way."

I suddenly knew who had interviewed her. "Her name wasn't Ellen Briar, by any chance, was it?"

Polly seemed to think about it, and then she nodded. "As a matter of fact, it was. How could you possibly know that?"

"It turns out that her brother was the one who tried to blackmail you," I said. It was the missing link that we'd been searching for. Evidently Morgan had found a way to dip into his sister's files, and I was going to make certain that she knew about it.

"That was Morgan Briar?" Polly asked.

"Didn't you recognize his picture in the paper?" Emma's dad had found Morgan's mug shot, and he'd blown it up for the newspaper article he'd written.

"I never saw him. He was just a shadowy voice on the phone, and I've been waiting for the other shoe to drop since he first called me. Somebody must have stopped him first, though."

"That's what Grace and I are trying to figure out," I said.

"Ladies, I appreciate what you're doing. I need to ask you a rather large favor. Would you keep my story to yourselves, at least for the time being?"

"Of course we will," Grace said. "You don't have to worry about Suzanne or me. George won't hear it from either one of us; I can promise you that."

"I know he won't, at least not from you. I'm going to tell him myself as soon as you leave."

"You don't have to share this with him," Grace said.

It was Polly's turn to pat *her* hand. "I know that. I want to, though. It's high time we were completely and utterly frank with one another. Speaking with the two of you, I've suddenly realized that it's the only way that either one of us is ever going to be able to move forward."

As she stood, Grace and I followed suit, and after we left her place, I reached for my cell phone.

"Who are you calling? Suzanne, you're not phoning George, are you?" Grace asked.

"No way. I'm staying as far away from that as I possibly can."

"Then who are you trying to reach?"

"I'm calling Ellen Briar. It's time she learned exactly what her brother was up to. If she wants any chance of making this right with any of us, she's going to have pitch in herself and get her hands a little dirty."

"What if she says no?" Grace asked me, but I held up one hand as I heard the Union Square police officer answer on the other end.

"Ellen, this is Suzanne Hart. We need to talk."

After a heavy sigh on the other end, Ellen said, "I've got nothing else to say to you, Suzanne. I thought I made that perfectly clear the last time that we spoke."

"Well then, the least that you can do is listen. I know where your brother got most of the information he was using to blackmail people."

"Where?"

"I'm guessing that must you keep a file cabinet at home full of unproven or weak cases you've worked on over the years. It's probably a hobby for you, isn't it? Why would you do that? Were you bucking to get off the desk and back out into the field?"

The woman wasn't slow on the uptake; I had to give her that. "Do you honestly think I'd let Morgan loose in my files? That cabinet's locked, Suzanne."

"And someone who's spent so much time in prison wouldn't learn how to overcome something like that, would he? Be realistic, Ellen. What would it hurt to see if I'm right? I'm willing to bet that if you go through those files right now, you'll see that I'm right on the money."

"Morgan wouldn't steal from me," she said resolutely.

"Would he even consider it stealing, given that they were just police files? You've *got* to let us search where he was staying. We could help you."

"No," Ellen said, and I could hear in her voice that there was no waffling at all. "I've looked through his things, and there's nothing like that anywhere."

I was about to tell her about the orange-handled key to the bus station locker when something made me hesitate. It might help her to know what she was looking for, but then again, what if she managed to find the evidence without us? How much of it would still be available to us then? I had no doubt that she'd do what she could to protect her brother's memory, even if it meant suppressing evidence in the blackmail case. It wasn't as though anybody would ever be prosecuted for it. Still, I decided to keep my mouth shut, just in case.

"Are you *sure* that you don't need any help?" I asked. "A couple of fresh sets of eyes might be in order. We're good at this, Ellen. Ask Chief Martin if you don't believe me."

"There's no need. He's already sung your praises to me, but that doesn't mean that I have to trust you. Good bye, Suzanne."

I closed my phone with a frown.

"*That* didn't go as well as you'd hoped, did it?" Grace asked me.

"I need to see her face-to-face," I said. "It's a lot harder to tell someone no when you're looking into their eyes."

"Then let's go to her house," Grace said.

"I'm game if you are. It's just half an hour to Union Square."

"And after we're finished, maybe we can grab a bite at Napoli's. They *have* to be open now, and I've been craving lasagna for weeks."

"Then that's what we'll do," I said. "Let's take the Jeep."

"That sounds good to me. That way I can nap on the drive over."

I studied Grace for a second, and then I asked, "Why are you so tired?"

"Hey, sleuthing is hard work."

"You don't have to tell me," I said with a grin. I would have hated investigating this case without Grace by my side. When things seemed at their darkest, she always managed to pick me up, just by being there. It was a trait more precious than diamonds to me. Well, not really big ones, but standard ones, anyway.

"She's not home," Grace said after I rang Ellen's doorbell for the third straight time with no response. The place was a little rundown, with weeds growing up against the house, and the siding was in dire need of a paint job. There were no cars in the driveway, and the repeated lack of response was another clue that Ellen wasn't there. The doghouse out front was in nice shape, though, with a new coat of paint, and the name SPIKE carefully labeled over the door, but if a dog lived there, he wasn't at home, either.

"We could just break in and look around for ourselves," I said as I studied the door lock for a moment.

"What if the dog's *inside*, instead of out here?" Grace asked.

"We'll deal with him when we run into him, then."

Grace put a hand on my shoulder and pulled me back up. "Suzanne Hart, as much as it pains me to say this, you've been hanging around with me too long. We're not going to break into the home of a police officer; do you hear me? Not even Jake's pull could get us out of the slammer if we got caught."

"That's a big 'if,' though," I said, and then I realized how foolish I was being. My decision to give up on the idea was more about Jake's certain disapproval than the possibility of being arrested. "Yeah, you're right. Let's go."

"That's excellent," Grace said. "I'm dying to eat at Napoli's."

"Me, too, but we're coming back here after we finish."

Grace frowned at me. "Don't you have a donut shop to run tomorrow?"

"I do, same as always, but that's not going to stop me from trying to clear my family's name. If I have to, I'll shut the place down completely until we get to the bottom of this."

"Something just occurred to me," Grace said. "We really haven't done much about tackling the hit-and-run that Morgan thought your dad was involved in. Is it possible that Morgan's death was tied into his brother's?"

I held up Jake's notebook. "I don't know, but that's why we've got this. If our leads start to run out on Morgan's murder, we'll start digging into my father's past. To be honest with you, I'm not all that thrilled about what we might uncover."

Grace hugged me as she said, "Suzanne, knowing is better than not knowing, ten out of ten times."

"I just hope that you're right," I replied as we got back into the Jeep and headed toward Napoli's.

If nothing else, we should get a nice meal out of it, and who knew? With any luck, we might just uncover a few leads in my boyfriend's investigative notebook as we ate. After we finished, though, we were coming straight back to Ellen Briar's home.

I had a hunch that there were answers there waiting for us, if only we could get in.

LEMON BANGS

We go through phases at my house where lemon is the absolute favorite flavor on the planet for us. When my significant other complained that I didn't make enough lemon donuts, I pulled out all of the stops on this one, even though I didn't have any fresh lemons on hand at the time. If I had, I would have added some zest to both the batter and the icing, and I would have added some juice as well, but these are still delicious just the way they are. Be warned. If you're not a huge lemon fan, you might want to cut back a little on the lemon extract, or even try something a little milder in taste, but for us, this recipe goes off with a bang!

INGREDIENTS

MIXED
1/2 cup whole milk (2% will do)
1 egg, lightly beaten
1 Tablespoon canola oil (any vegetable oil will do)
1 1/2 teaspoons lemon extract

SIFTED
1 cup flour, unbleached all-purpose
1/2 cup sugar, granulated
1 teaspoon baking soda
1/4 teaspoon nutmeg
1/4 teaspoon cinnamon
1/4 teaspoon salt

ICING
1/2 cup confectioner's sugar
1 Tablespoon warm water
1/2 teaspoon lemon extract

INSTRUCTIONS

If you're using your oven, preheat to 365 degrees F before you start mixing.
In a bowl, beat the egg lightly, then add the milk, canola oil, and lemon extract. In a separate bowl, sift together the flour, sugar, baking soda, nutmeg, cinnamon, and salt. Add the dry ingredients to the wet, mixing well until you have a smooth consistency.
Put the batter into your donut pans or into your donut baker and bake for eight to ten minutes in your oven, five to six minutes in your donut baker, or until they're richly brown.

Yield 10-12 small donuts

Lemon Icing

Mix 1/2 cup confectioner's sugar, 1 Tablespoon warm water, and 1/2 teaspoon lemon extract. Mix until it's combined, and then drizzle on top of the donuts while they are still warm.

Chapter 13

"This lasagna is so good it should be illegal," Grace said as she took another bite. I had ordered my usual ravioli, something I really loved, but she was bragging about her meal so much that I had to have some.

"Can I have a bite before it's all gone?" I asked.

Grace stared down at her plate, and then she looked critically at me. "Suzanne, I've been known to stab a date's hand when they were reaching for my food, but I'll share with you. Just a little bite, though, okay?"

"Thanks," I said as I took some of the lasagna and tasted it. There was an explosion of cheeses, sauce, and pasta in my mouth, and I was beginning to regret my ravioli choice. "That is unbelievable," I replied.

Angelica was standing nearby, watching over the restaurant's dining room like a mother hen. I motioned her over, but she held up one finger and vanished into the kitchen. I just wanted to tell her how great the food was, but evidently it was going to have to wait.

That's when she reappeared with a fresh plate full of lasagna.

"This is for you," she said as she slid the new offering beside my plate.

"I couldn't possibly eat all of that," I said as I looked at the mound of food.

"I can help," Grace said with a greedy smile.

"Angelica, I'd really love to dive into this, but I'm nearly full now."

"That's not a problem," she said with a big grin. "Eat what you want, and then you can take the rest home with you. Should I go ahead and put it in a container to go?"

I looked at the plate of lasagna again, and then I said with a smile, "Not just yet. I'm sure I can eat a little. Just put it on my tab, okay?"

Angela's smile dissipated quickly. She had a heart as big as the world, but she was not a woman to be crossed. "We've already discussed this, Suzanne. Tonight's meal is with our compliments. You're not going to spoil my evening and argue with me, are you? Who climbed up on my roof when no one else would?"

"It wasn't all that big a deal," I said.

"To you, maybe not, but to me and my girls, yes, it was. Now, if you keep arguing with me, you're getting three desserts to take home with you, too."

"Three? But there are only two of us," I said.

"I think we can handle it," Grace said.

"The third is for your mother," Angelica said. "I'm sure she'd enjoy it."

"I'm done arguing," I said happily. "You win. Just the lasagna, though."

"Plus the desserts," Angelica added.

I knew when I was outmatched, and besides, I really didn't want to win that particular argument in the first place. Instead, I stood and hugged her.

Angelica was no dainty flower. When she hugged me back, I could almost feel a few ribs start to crack. "Thank you," I whispered.

"Suzanne, you are very welcome," Angelica said. "Now, I'll leave you ladies to finish your meals, and when you're ready, just let me know and I'll have one of the girls wrap all of this up for you, including the desserts."

After the restaurant owner was gone, I took a knife and cut off a small portion of the lasagna and slid it onto my plate. After I'd done that, I looked at Grace and asked, "Are you sure you want more right now?"

"No," she said with real regret in her voice. "I'm afraid that my eyes are too big for my stomach. It's going to be tough enough as it is to eat dessert."

"Grace, you're kidding, right? You actually have room for something else?"

"Not at the moment, but I have high hopes for later," she

said.

I took the few bites I'd set aside, and I felt the rush of good food wash over me like a rain shower. I knew that all of the owner's girls were good at preparing food for the restaurant, but this had the teacher's touch, and there was no doubt in my mind that it had come from Angelica's own hands. I tried to take another bite, it was that good, but finally I pushed the plate away. "I'm going to explode if I try to go on."

Grace nodded. "I'm miserable, too, but I'm happy. That woman is a wonder in the kitchen, isn't she?"

"I think they all are," I agreed.

Angelica saw that we'd thrown in the towel, and she hurried over to us with a large tray. "I'll have these ready in no time, but feel free to linger all you'd like. Maria will be by with two coffees in a moment."

"Thanks again, for everything," I said.

"Enough thanks. This is my pleasure," she said.

Maria was at our table ten seconds after Angelica walked back into the kitchen, and she delivered two cups of luxurious coffee.

"Your mother is spoiling us," I said. "And to make matters worse, she won't let us pay for our dinners tonight."

"Suzanne, we've known each other a long time. Do you trust me?" the beautiful young woman asked.

"You know that I do," I answered.

"Then take it and smile. My mother gets great pleasure doing this, and I'd hate for you to rob her of it."

"We wouldn't dream of it," Grace said.

After Maria was gone, I took a sip of the coffee. It was the perfect end to a rather spectacular meal. "Wow, that's great, too," Grace said. "Is there *anything* those ladies can't do?"

"Well, at least I can climb ladders better than they can," I said with a smile.

"And aren't we both glad that's true," Grace replied. Her smile quickly faded, though, as she continued, "Did you have any idea how bad Polly's husband's condition got at the end of his life?"

"No, she somehow managed to keep that a secret. I doubt that even Momma knew, and she's got more sources in town than Ray Blake." Emma's dad was good at running our newspaper, but he couldn't match my mother's list of contacts, and what's more, he knew it. "Can you believe that Morgan tried to blackmail her about what happened?"

"When it comes to that man, I'd believe just about anything," Grace said. "He had some nerve, going through his sister's files like that. I wouldn't be all that surprised to find that he tried to blackmail a dozen more people that we don't even know about."

"You're probably right, as long as they were all women. That's the pattern we've found so far, anyway. He was quite a coward, wasn't he?"

"Foolish, I'd say. A man might punch you in the nose on the spur of the moment, but it would take a woman to do a better job of it and not stop with something that mild. I don't know who called us the weaker sex, but they were dead wrong as far as I'm concerned."

"I have a hunch that Morgan learned that particular lesson just fine all by himself," I said. Jake's notebook was in my pocket, and I'd been dying for the right chance to take it out and *really* study it. I looked at Grace as I took it out and I asked, "Should we take this somewhere else so we can read it a little more carefully?"

My best friend looked around the crowded restaurant. "I don't believe that a single soul here is paying any attention to us."

I had to agree as I studied the room myself. "Let's see what Jake has to say, then," I said as I opened it.

The first page was headed, "Morgan and Blake Briar Murder/Death Investigations", and the second had a list of suspects for each event, most names still clear, and only one crossed out. As I read them aloud, Grace took it all in. I stumbled a little when I got to my own father's name, and I was unhappy to see that it hadn't been the one that had been crossed out. That one was Morgan Briar. Had Jake really considered him a suspect in his own brother's death all those years ago? I wasn't sure that I would have added him to my list, but I was positive that Jake had his reasons. I didn't know three of the other names, but Grace and I would have to start digging into them before long.

"He's pretty thorough, isn't he?" Grace asked as she looked at the book upside down. "What's on the next page?"

I turned to the one in question and read, "Motives To Consider. Money and Greed." Below that was another line, with the captions, "Hide something, Expose something, Protect something, Steal something, Get Revenge for something."

There was nothing under any of these listings, and the rest of the pages of the book were blank.

"He didn't get very far, did he?" Grace asked as she took the book from me and leafed through the pages again herself.

"We didn't exactly give him much time," I said, automatically defending him.

Grace threw her hands into the air. "Hey, I wasn't accusing him of anything. I'm just saying that we've got our work cut out for us if we're going to solve two murders."

"One murder and one possible accident," I reminded her.

"Doesn't it make more sense if someone killed Blake on purpose?" she asked.

"To be honest with you, I'm not sure *what* makes sense at this point. What if the two events have nothing in common except that they both happened to Briar brothers? If Blake was an accident, it could be totally unrelated to what happened to Morgan. He was a blackmailer, remember?"

"Well," Grace said after a moment's pause, "not to make too fine a point of it, but they can't be *totally* unrelated."

"What else links them?" I asked.

"Your dad," she said with a hushed voice.

"He didn't do it," I said loudly.

"Hey, take it easy," Grace said softly. "No one's accusing

him of anything, but Morgan had that letter, didn't he?"

"It doesn't prove anything. I'd love to know where that key to the locker at the bus station is. I've got a hunch that all of the answers are in there."

"Suzanne, I hate to bring this up, but that key might not even matter anymore."

"What are you talking about, Grace?"

"What if Morgan moved whatever he'd been storing there, and it's someplace else entirely now?"

I shook my head. "That way of thinking doesn't do our investigation any good. We have to assume that there's a key out there somewhere that is protecting the answers that we need, and until I find out that it's not true, I'm going to believe it with all of my heart."

"Then we look for the key," Grace said. "You know, I'm beginning to wonder if you might have been right earlier."

"Really? That's certainly refreshing. Would you care to tell me more, so I have a better chance of repeating the result in the future?"

Grace grinned at me, and then she said, "Stop fishing for compliments. You know how good you are at this. I'm just wondering if we should have broken into Ellen's place after all. If that key is anywhere, I've got a hunch that it's somewhere in her house."

"I agree, but if you'd heard the way she talked to me earlier, you wouldn't be suggesting that we burglarize her place. I don't know for a fact that she'd shoot first and ask questions later, but I for one don't want to find out. The *only* way that we're going to be able to search that place is at her invitation, and I'm not holding my breath waiting for one."

"Then what should we do next?" Grace asked.

I glanced at my watch, surprised by just how late it had gotten to be, at least by my standards. "I think we should both go home, sleep on it, and then see what we can come up with tomorrow. Are you ready to go?"

"Just as soon as we get our doggy bags and those desserts," she said.

"Are we seriously going to take food home with you after all you just ate?"

"Don't let there be a single doubt in your mind."

As we drove back to April Springs, I couldn't help wondering if tomorrow would bring us any closer to the truth than we were at that moment. It was frustrating beyond belief trying to work on two cases so many years apart. I didn't know how Jake ever managed it, and I wished that we still had him with us.

But he had his hands full at the moment fighting his own demons. I wondered if he'd made any progress on tracking down the bomber yet, but I knew if the terrorist could be found, Jake would do his best to be a part of it.

It was just beginning to get dark when we pulled into April Springs, and I was looking at the clock where Morgan had been murdered when Grace poked my arm.

"What is it?" I asked as I pivoted to face her.

"Is that who I think it is?" she asked.

I turned to see Max and Emily walking down the street holding hands and chatting about something. Emily smiled when my ex-husband said something, and I could see why he was so earnestly pursuing her. There was something about the woman that was enchanting, and for once, it appeared that *Max* was the one who was mesmerized.

"You're not jealous, are you?" Grace asked me as we drove past them, offering a quick wave as we did so.

"Not even a little bit," I said. "Maybe it's because I have Jake in my life now, but I don't think that's all of it. The truth is that I don't hate Max anymore, and I've always been a huge fan of Emily's. If they can manage to find each other in this crazy world, more power to them both."

As I pulled in front of Grace's place, she asked, "You really mean that, don't you?"

"It's taken me a while, but I finally got there."

"I'm so proud of you," she said with a laugh. "My little baby's growing up."

"Go on," I said with a laugh. "You'd better jump out

before I make you walk home from my place."

Since that was all of a hundred yards, it wasn't really that much of a threat.

Grace got out, and then she leaned forward. "I'll see you around eleven."

"Tomorrow morning, right?"

"Well, I'm not waking you up tonight. Go home, get some sleep, and let's figure out how we should tackle this tomorrow."

"It's a deal."

When I got home, Momma was on the couch reading another mystery. I was surprised, though, to see that it was the choice of my book club meeting tomorrow. I'd nearly forgotten all about it with so much real murder in the air, but at least I'd read it earlier. "How do you like it so far?" I asked Momma as I dead-bolted the front door behind me.

"This constantly changing point of view is kind of confusing," she admitted as she closed the book and studied the cover. "Are all of her books like this?"

"I don't know. This is the first one that I've read, and probably the last. I'm sure some people love her, but she's just not my taste."

"Agreed," Momma said as she set the book aside.

I was flabbergasted. "You're not going to finish it anyway?" I asked her. I'd never known my mother to cast a book away, no matter how bad it might be, until she was finished with it.

"I'm not getting any younger, Suzanne," she said with a smile. "I don't have time to read the books I *want* to read, let alone force myself to drag through something like this."

"Fair enough," I said as I reached for it to take to bed with me.

"You're not going to leave it here?" she asked with a hint of desperation in her voice.

"I thought that you were finished with it," I said, not even trying to hide my grin.

"Oh, give it back," she said with a frown. "Maybe it will get better." I handed the book back to her as she asked, "Will it?"

"That's only for you to say," I answered as I kissed her forehead. "Good night, Momma."

"Good night, Angel," she said. Momma certainly didn't have cause to call me that very many times, especially after I hit the terrible twos, but it gave me the warmest glow whenever I heard it.

"I love you," I said from the top of the stairs. "You know that, don't you?"

"It's something I count on each and every day," Momma answered. "I trust you know that I feel the same way about you."

"If there's one thing in this world that I'm sure of when everything around me is going crazy, it's that you love me."

"Good," she said.

As I disappeared up the stairs, the last thing I saw was her getting back to the book in question, a frown on her face accompanied by a look of determination that I knew all too well.

One way or the other, Momma was finishing that book tonight, even if she had to stay up until I left for work to do it.

Chapter 14

I was mashing bananas the next morning at the shop for my latest donut creation, one I was going to call Banana Split, when Emma came into the kitchen from the dining room. "Suzanne, somebody's out front knocking on the door."

"Who is it?" I asked as I wiped my hands on a nearby towel.

"I've never seen her before in my life. All I know is that she's a cop *I* don't recognize."

"I'll take care of it," I said, knowing exactly who it had to be. I hurried out to see what Ellen wanted. The last time we'd spoken, she hadn't been all that happy with me. Was she coming back to give me more grief, or had she had a sudden change of heart?

"Good morning," I said as I unlocked the front door for her. "I'm sorry, but we don't have any donuts ready yet. Would you like some coffee?"

"Sure, that would be great," she said. "Suzanne, we need to talk."

"Give me one second, okay? I'll be right back."

"That's fine."

I walked into the kitchen, and Emma asked me, "Who is she?"

"Can you do me a favor? I need a recipe out of my book, but I left mine at home. Could you get your mother's copy for me?"

"Right now?" she asked.

"If you don't mind." I had to get her out of there so that Ellen and I would be free to talk.

"Suzanne, do you *really* need your book, or are you just trying to get rid of me?"

There was only one way that I could answer such a direct question. "Honestly? I need some privacy for this particular conversation," I explained to her.

"What if I promise to stay in the kitchen with my iPod turned up to its highest setting? I promise that I won't eavesdrop on you, but I've got work here that I can be doing, so there's no sense in me leaving. You trust me, don't you?"

I nodded. "I do, but that's not the point. I know that you promised me that you wouldn't share anything you learned here with your father without my permission."

"And you can believe it," Emma said. "I lost my place here once. It's not going to happen again. When you made room for me again after my brief college fling, I told Dad that his source at the donut shop was gone for good."

"The problem is that this is kind of sensitive," I said. "If you're working back here, she might not open up to me, and I need her candor a lot more than I can explain."

"That's all that I need to hear. When should I come back?"

"I'll call you on my cell phone when we're finished," I said as I led Emma back out front. My assistant smiled at Ellen on her way out, and then I let her out into the darkness. I wasn't sure if she was going home or just to her car, but I appreciated her agreeing to my odd request.

"Where's she going?" Ellen asked as I locked the door behind Emma.

"I wanted us to have some privacy for our chat," I admitted. "We're completely alone now, so you can say whatever you'd like to me without worrying about someone listening in from the other room."

"That's good," the police officer said, and I could see her shoulders ease a little.

"What brings you by here so early?" I asked as I poured us both coffees. "Are you getting off your shift, or just getting ready to start it?"

"I don't start until seven," she said, "but I haven't been able to sleep after our conversation last night."

"I didn't mean to wreck your night," I said. "And if I was rude, it wasn't my intention. I understand that you are just trying to protect your brother. Or his memory, at any rate."

"That's just it," Ellen said as she pushed her mug around on the table without drinking much of it. "There's nothing that needs to be salvaged. I know that my brother was *anything* but reformed while he was in prison. Nothing you told me surprised me, but I still didn't want to believe it."

"What changed your mind?" I asked.

"I checked my file cabinet when I got home, and I discovered that someone had pried it open with a letter opener. He didn't even try to pick the lock. I could still see the scratches from where he got in."

"Was anything missing?" I asked her, holding my breath a little as I did.

"Four files were gone," she said, her heart clearly heavy from making the admission.

"I'm willing to bet that I can name the people who were mentioned in those reports." I recited the folks I knew who were being blackmailed, and Ellen reluctantly nodded her agreement.

"Is that why you're here?" I asked.

"I think you have a right to look around Morgan's things," she answered. "I was going to do it myself, but I couldn't stand the thought of finding more evidence of what has already taken me too long to accept. Your chief of police has looked it over, but you might be able to find something that he missed. The more eyes looking the better, and if you come up empty, it's no great loss. After the way Morgan tried to treat you, you at least deserve the chance to see for yourself." Ellen paused a moment, and then she asked me, "You close at eleven, is that right?"

"On the nose," I agreed.

"Well, I'll be there at twelve thirty to eat my lunch, and if you and your friend are both gone before I get there, just leave my keys in the mailbox. Nobody's going to steal from a cop; not if they know what's good for them. That should give you an hour, if you take out the travel time. I hope it's enough, because it's all that I can give you."

"That should be perfect," I said. "Thanks so much for doing this."

"You're welcome. Just don't make me regret my decision. I don't want you to take anything without telling me about it first. If you happen to find anything of interest, I expect you to hang around until I get there. Agreed?"

"Agreed," I said readily. "What if I close the shop early? Can we start exploring then?"

"One hour," she said as she held up one finger.

"Okay. Got it." I looked at Ellen's coffee, and I saw that she hadn't taken a sip of it yet. "Is that all right? I could freshen it for you if you'd like."

"No, I really can't. My allergies are killing me, and coffee just seems to make them worse."

"I sneeze sometimes myself when August gets here," I conceded.

"Mine are year-round. I'm allergic to pollen, peanuts, milk, the dander from dogs and cats, dust, latex, and a host of other things. It's a real pain, let me tell you."

"I can sympathize," I said.

Ellen stood up, and I walked her to the door as she reached for her keys, which were attached to her belt. They slipped off too easily, and she fumbled with them for a second before she caught them. "I've *got* to get a new clip for these. They keep slipping off my belt." I took them from her and tucked her keys into my jeans pocket. "Thanks for doing this, Ellen. I know how hard it must be on you."

"We all have to deal with family issues, don't we?"

I wasn't exactly sure how to answer that, so I just shrugged. It was pretty clear that she was referring to my father, but I wasn't about to address that issue with her.

As soon as the police officer from Union Square was gone, I grabbed my cell phone and hit Emma's speed dial button.

"Hello?"

"It's safe to come back now. Are you at home?"

"Nope, I'm just out in my car. I didn't mean to nap, but I

think I drifted off there for a second."

"Sorry about that," I said.

"Are you kidding me? I just got paid for taking a nap." She hesitated, and then she asked, "I *will* get paid for that time, won't I?"

I had to laugh. "You bet. Come on back in, and we'll get back to business."

"See you soon, Boss," she said.

Emma was as good as her word, and less than a minute later, I let her back into the shop. I looked into the bowl where I'd been mashing bananas and I realized that I hadn't taken the time to dip the bananas in lemon juice before I started. They were now an unappetizing brown mush, so I chucked the contents of the bowl and grabbed three more bananas. After slicing them, I dipped each one into the lemon juice, and then I smashed the contents into a paste. That was incorporated into some of my cake donut mix, along with a handful of chocolate chips and chopped maraschino cherries. I'd played with the idea of adding a little marshmallow as well, but so far I hadn't had the guts to do it. I wasn't sure how that marshmallow fluff would react to being deep fried, so I'd avoided it so far. As we worked at preparing the day's offerings, I couldn't help but wonder what Grace and I might find in Morgan's room at Ellen's place. Was he stupid enough to leave something incriminating in sight, or had he been crafty finding a place to protect everyone else's secrets? Only time would tell, but I had a hunch that Grace and I would have our hands full with just an hour allowed for our search.

"Young lady, we need to talk," George Morris said later that morning as I opened the door to Donut Hearts promptly at six.

"Hello, Mr. Mayor," I said as I let him inside. From the expression on his face and his tone of voice, I had a hunch that my friend wasn't there to try one of my new donuts.

"What's going on with your investigation?" he asked.

"I take it that you've talked to your secretary."

"We both know that she's more than that to me. Polly is an important part of my life these days, and I don't care who knows it."

"Well, good for you," I said with a smile as I put a hand on his chest. "I'm proud of you."

"For being mayor?" he asked.

"No, for admitting that you have a girlfriend."

George frowned. "I hate the term girlfriend. We both retired from long careers, and we had full lives before we ever met. It just doesn't sound dignified calling Polly my girlfriend."

"I can think of some other terms of endearment, but I doubt that you'll like any of them any better."

"No, I'm certain that you're right, but my question stands. Have you made any progress finding Morgan Briar's killer?"

I poured him a cup of coffee and grabbed one of his favorite plain cake donuts and plated it for him. "Why don't you sit down, and we'll talk about it?"

"I suppose that we *can* speak uninterrupted. You're not exactly busy at the moment," George said as he looked around the deserted donut shop.

"The heat seems to keep people away in droves," I admitted. "But maybe this morning that's a good thing. George, you know that I love you, but you need to stay as far away from this case as you can."

"I was a cop once upon a time," he said, as if I needed to be reminded.

"And now you're the mayor. It's a lot different, and you know it. Grace and I are doing everything in our power to get this all cleared up, but there's nothing you can do to help us that might not reflect badly on you if folks found out."

"I don't care *who* knows what I do," he snapped. George had a great heart, but sometimes his temper had a bit of a bite.

"Well, maybe you should," I said gently, hoping to lower his blood pressure a few notches if I remained calm. "You're going to want to *keep* being mayor after your term is up, aren't you?"

"I don't honestly know," he said. "Sometimes I think the headaches aren't worth it."

I knew for a fact that George loved his job most of the time, and that he was speaking out of frustration right now. "Does that mean that you aren't going to run again?"

George frowned at his coffee, took a sip, and then he said, "Of course I'm running again. I've never felt so useful since I retired. I know that I used to help you with your investigations, but it was never a fulltime job for me."

"Believe me, no one wants you to run for reelection more than I do, but in order to keep your job, you have to be careful how you are perceived. With Polly involved, it can go all kinds of ways wrong for you."

"That's just it, though," he said after taking a bite of his donut. "Nobody knows she's a part of this mess except for you and Grace."

"And whoever the blackmailer might have told before he died."

"That's the thing, though, isn't it? Polly told me everything that happened with her late husband, and she didn't do anything wrong, not legally or ethically. Morgan was going after the wrong mark when he focused on her."

"Is *everyone* going to feel that way if they hear about what happened? You know the folks who live in this town as well as I do. Tongues will wag; you can be sure of it. Right now, Grace and I are trying to keep a low profile investigating, but if you get involved, the attention's going to really step up, and what's more, I think you know that as well as I do."

The mayor frowned, and then he rotated his neck a little trying to clear out some of the tension in it. "Yeah, I suppose you're right. It's just so frustrating having to stand on the sidelines while you do all the work."

"And hog all of the fun too, right?" I asked.

"There's not much that's amusing about this."

"I know that the crimes have been atrocious, but I don't have to tell you about the satisfaction you feel when you catch the bad guy."

"You've got the bug now, don't you?" he asked with a smile.

"What are you talking about?" I asked as I grabbed another donut for him. One was usually his limit, but this was not a typical day, and I thought he could use a little more of the TLC that my comfort food provided.

"You *like* digging into murder."

"Like I said, I like the fact that the bad guys have to pay for their actions," I replied.

"Solve this one, Suzanne."

"We're doing our best."

"I know that you are." He took a five from his wallet, and then he pointed to the second donut I'd just given him. "Put that one in a bag and I'll eat it at my desk."

As I bagged the second donut, I asked, "Won't Polly fuss at you for having it?" She was well known around town for keeping him from indulging too much.

"She's not coming in today," George replied. "As a matter of fact, she's taking some time off until things settle down. This has all brought up a lot of bad memories for her, and she needs some time to deal with it in her own way."

"I'm so sorry," I said. "I hope that Grace and I didn't make things worse with her."

"No apology necessary. Polly told me that if it weren't for the two of you confronting her like that, she might have melted down from the stress of it all. Telling the two of you all about it was cathartic for her, and by the time she filled me in, she was starting to get a handle on it. Sure, she shed a few tears, but the odd thing was that as soon as her crying jag ended, she felt instantly better. If I live to be a hundred, I'll never understand that woman."

"That's all a part of the fun of it, isn't it?"

"Maybe, maybe not," George said as he headed for the door. "Keep me informed," he said with a grin, "or I'll have every parking space within a mile of this place changed to a 'no parking zone.'"

"Wow, that's just plain mean," I answered with a smile of my own.

"Good luck," my friend said, and then he headed out the door as a pair of men in suits walked into the shop. I held my breath as they approached, wondering if their visit had anything to do with Morgan Briar's murder. Fortunately, I was soon relieved to learn that they just wanted two coffees to go.

"I wanted to love this book; I really did," Jennifer said a little later as my book club gathered at our favorite couch in Donut Hearts. "The cover was really well done, the description on the back was intriguing, and the first chapter was wonderful, too. I'm afraid she lost me soon after that, though." There was just the four of us in the club, but we always had a good time discussing our latest pick.

"I know exactly what you mean," Elizabeth answered. "I'm so sorry. The author was so nice, really funny, and just plain charming, that I may have read it with my rose-colored glasses on."

"Do you correspond with her online, too?" I asked. Elizabeth loved emailing authors, and I was always really surprised by how many actually responded.

"No. She stays away from the Internet entirely, at least as far as I've been able to determine. The Facebook page she has was created by her publisher, and there's not even any way to contact her on her website."

"That's odd these days, isn't it?" Hazel asked as she picked at her donut. She was constantly on a diet, but you'd never know it by the way she ate during our meetings.

"It's just about unheard of," Elizabeth confirmed.

"You know what?" I asked. "I don't care if they hide in a cave and never come out, just as long as they keep writing good books that I enjoy. All of this emphasis on social media has to take a toll on them, and I have to believe that it hurts the books they write. I wonder how much harder it must be to keep focused on what's really important if you spend all of your time twittering and blogging online."

"It's called tweeting," Elizabeth corrected me.

Jennifer was curious now. "If she stays off the Internet, how do you know about her personality?"

"I'm certain that you all remember that I attended Malice Domestic last year," she said, something she loved bringing up whenever the opportunity arose. The conference was for mystery lovers and writers, and in Elizabeth's opinion, we all owed ourselves a trip to next year's conference.

"Of course," Hazel said. "Did you meet her there? Was she on a panel?"

"Actually, we had breakfast together," Elizabeth said, preening a little.

"And you never mentioned this before?" I asked, shocked by her reluctance to drop even the tiniest name in mystery writers.

"Well, I was so overwhelmed by the other authors present that I didn't even realize she was a writer until I ran across her latest novel at the bookstore."

"She jumps around an awful lot in this, doesn't she?" I ventured. "I found myself reading this book with a notepad handy just so I could keep track of who the characters were, and what they were up to."

"I thought that it should have been at least twice as long as it was," Hazel said.

"What? You're kidding, right?" I asked. I was glad that I hadn't been drinking coffee when she'd said it, or I would have drenched the other three.

"She couldn't have made it any shorter," Hazel said, "without taking out half the characters and dropping the scenes in London entirely."

Jennifer seemed to think about it, and then she nodded. "The more that I think about it, that's exactly what she should have done. Did she even *have* an editor for this book? I understand it when a publisher is reluctant to interfere with a bestseller's book, but this was no bestseller."

"I don't know," I said. "Can you imagine trying to sort

this mess out, even if you're a professional at it? I'm
wondering why they published it at all."

"It's beyond me," Hazel said, and then she must have
realized how it sounded. "Maybe we're just not the right
audience for this one."

"Maybe," I agreed reluctantly. "So, Elizabeth, who else
was at your breakfast table at Malice?"

We spent the rest of the meeting chatting about our
favorite writers, and according to Elizabeth, almost none of
them actually looked like the photographs on their book
jackets, web sites, and publicity shots. It was great fun, and
as always, I was thrilled with the opportunity to get away
from my own life and worries for a little while and share my
time with such nice women. It had been my lucky day when
they'd first stumbled into my donut shop looking for a place
to hold their meeting. They'd taken me in immediately, and
I'd never regretted the time I'd spent joining them since.

Chapter 15

"Jake, I wasn't sure when I'd hear from you!" I said with delight as I answered my cell phone at the front counter later that morning. I normally would have had to think twice about taking the call if I'd been waiting on someone, but thankfully the customers I had visiting Donut Hearts at the moment were all enjoying their donuts, milk, and coffee. That's not entirely the truth, though. I would have answered this call anyway, *after* apologizing to my customer, and calling Emma up front, because it was Jake.

"Do you have a second to talk?" he asked. He sounded tired, and I wondered if he was getting any sleep at all.

"For you? Anytime. How's it going?"

"Slowly," he said, the weight of the investigation clearly taking some of the joy out of his voice. "The Governor's getting frustrated. So are the rest of us, for that matter."

"How's your boss doing?" I asked.

"He must be getting better; he's already fussed at me twice this morning. The man's cranky, but I can't blame him. If I were in his place, I'd be itching to get out into the field myself."

"I bet he's happy that you're there."

"If he is," Jake said, and I could hear the smile creep in his voice as he spoke, "he's doing a masterful job of hiding it. Anything new on your front?"

I brought him up to date on what had been happening, not mentioning my free meal at Napoli's, or the lack of help we'd gotten from his notebook.

He did it for me, though.

"Have you had a chance to look at my notes?"

"Just a quick glance," I said, not wanting to complain about its lack of useful information.

"Don't bother with it," he said. "On the drive to Raleigh,

I've come up with your next move, and it has nothing to do with anything that I wrote."

"How did you get the idea?" I asked, honestly curious about how he worked. Grace and I investigated by the seats of our pants, going from clue to clue and basically following our instincts along the way. Jake, on the other hand, was a seasoned investigator, who worked cases methodically until he cracked them wide open.

"Honestly, it didn't occur to me until I had time to reflect on something that I'd heard earlier. You need to find a man named Fred Harmon. I'm beginning to think that he's the key to what happened to Blake Briar all those years ago. I keep thinking that if we tie that death up, it will lead us to Morgan's killer."

"Why do you believe that?"

"Call it a cop's intuition," Jake said. "By the way, well done. That was a real breakthrough getting Ellen to let you search her brother's things. It must have been hard for her to do."

"I'm sure that it was. I was willing to go over there early, but she told me that I had to follow her timetable, or not go at all. I just hope there's something there. We have a few minor leads at this point, but nothing staggering."

"Suzanne, you know how these things usually work," he said. "You just have to keep pounding until you're able to come up with something you can use."

"That's what we're doing," I said.

"Listen, there's one more thing... Hang on." He covered the phone with his hand, but I could still hear some of his conversation. As though from a distance, I heard him tell someone else, "Yes, sir. Absolutely. I understand. I'll take care of it right away." Then he removed his hand and got back to me. "Sorry. I have to go."

I found myself staring at my dead telephone, wondering what Jake had been about to add, and even more, I was curious about who had just given him that order, and what it was about. My boyfriend was definitely traveling in more important circles on this case than he usually did.

I just hoped that someone higher up didn't take a liking to him and steal him for themselves. Jake's current schedule suited us just fine, and I hated the thought of him being tied down somewhere like Raleigh. My shop was open seven days a week, and my weekends were usually my busiest times, so it wouldn't bode well for us if he had to make that commute every weekend. Oh, well. I wouldn't worry about that unless it became reality.

At the moment, I had plenty of problems of my own without adding phantom ones to the mix.

"Excuse me. Are you Suzanne Hart?" a man asked me as I locked the front door of the shop, chalking up another day of making and selling donuts. He was a large fellow, with hands that looked as though they could squeeze water out of granite.

"I am," I said feeling suddenly nervous as I put my keys between my fingers to use as a weapon if I needed to fight back. I ordinarily wasn't that paranoid, but working on a murder case had a habit of doing that to me.

"I'm Cliff Gentry. Heather Morningstar told me about you."

"What can I do for you, Mr. Gentry?" The last thing I wanted to do was tip him off about what Heather had discussed with me.

"It's Cliff. And don't worry. I know everything."

I still wasn't sure that I should believe him. "Would you care to explain what you mean by 'everything'?"

Cliff grinned at me. "My, you don't give up *anything*, do you? Would you like to call her and check up on me?" He'd been joking, but I wasn't.

"As a matter of fact, that's a great idea." I took out my cell and dialed Heather's number.

"Cliff's here," I said after we said our hellos. "He says he knows everything. Is that true?"

"It is," she said, the relief clear in her voice. "You can talk to him about anything he asks you about."

"Okay. I just wanted to check with you first."

"Angelica was right about you," Heather said with the hint of a laugh in her voice. "You really *are* a woman of your word, aren't you?"

"If I don't have my honor, what do I have?" I asked.

After I hung up, I turned to Cliff and smiled. "Now that that's settled, what can I do for you?"

"I'm just touching base to see if you've been able to come up with anything. Heather broke down and told me what happened just after you two spoke. I've got you to thank for that, and I can't tell you how much I appreciate it."

"I'm happy that I could help, but I'm afraid there's nothing new to report at this point."

Cliff nodded, and then he said, "May I call you Suzanne?"

"You may," I said, smiling at his comfortable way with people.

"Suzanne, I don't know if Heather said anything to you, but I'm a man of certain means. If there's anything that cash can accomplish, I'm more than willing to kick in. No limit, if I think it's called for."

Wow, could this man really afford to make that kind of offer? He clearly loved and cared about Heather.

"As much as I appreciate the gesture, that's not the way I work. I get most of my information from folks who trust me, and the kind of people I talk to would be offended if I took out my checkbook."

"I understand that, but there are times when a little persuasion is required. No, that's not right. Maybe incentive would be a better word for it."

"I get it. If I need any inducements, I'll give Heather a call, and she can get in touch with you."

Cliff frowned as he handed me his business card. "If it's all the same to you, I'd rather you phone me directly. That number is the best way to reach me."

I took the card and felt the rich texture of the stock, and ran a finger across the raised burgundy letters printed on a cream field. "I will." As he started to walk away, I asked, "I take it the wedding is still on?"

"It would take a great deal more than this past indiscretion for me to change my mind. Heather is the love of my life. I won't hold her responsible for something that happened long before I ever met her."

"Cliff, you're quite the catch, if you don't mind my saying so."

"Because of the cash?" he asked.

I looked long and hard with him before I spoke. "Is that what you really think?"

Cliff studied me in turn for a moment, and then he said, "Of course not. It was nice meeting you, Suzanne."

"You, too."

"Listen, if you'd be at all interested, we'd love to have you come to our wedding. I know that Heather would be delighted."

I had too much work to do with this case to drop everything and start socializing with my suspects. "Tell you what. If we catch the killer in two days, Grace and I will be there."

"Is she your... partner?" he asked delicately.

"Actually, she's my best friend. I have a hunch that I couldn't get my boyfriend to come with me under gunpoint. Besides, he's got a case that he's working on himself."

"Nevertheless, if he can free up some time, you're all welcome."

"Thanks again."

As Cliff headed off to a limousine that I hadn't noticed before, Grace walked up and joined me on the sidewalk. "Who was that?" she asked as Cliff got into the back.

"He's Heather Morningstar's fiancé," I said.

Grace frowned. "Does he know what happened?"

"Knows it, forgives it, and has offered to support us financially to fix it."

"He must be quite a guy," she said as the car pulled away.

"He invited you, Jake, and me to the wedding."

"What did you say?"

"I told him that if we were able to find the murderer in time, we'd be delighted."

Grace grinned at me. "You and I might be happy to go, but I doubt that Jake will be all that pleased about the invitation."

"Then you and I will go together."

"In the meantime," Grace said, "Shall we go to Ellen's place and start digging?"

I glanced at my watch. "We'd better hustle. We're on a tight schedule, remember?"

"Maybe I'd better drive," she said.

"You're on."

As we neared Ellen's place, I pointed to the side of the road and said, "There it is, remember? Pull in by the doghouse."

Grace did as I instructed, and as we got out, I touched the roof of the doghouse with one hand. Whoever had spruced the canine domicile up should have used the paint on the house instead. The shutters were peeling, and the faded wooden siding was showing some serious signs of disrepair.

"Boy, she's really not much for maintenance around here, is she?" Grace asked.

"The dog lives better than she does. Let's go in and see what we can find." I took the keys Ellen had given me and unlocked the three locks she had on her front door. "It appears that she spent her budget on security for this place."

I opened the locks, one after the other, and the door swung open. I didn't go in just yet, though. I stood there for a second, poised to slam it. "Here, Spike. Here, boy."

There was no response inside.

"It appears to be safe," I said as Grace and I walked in together.

"I know for one that *I'm* relieved. Let's find Morgan's room and start digging."

It was the second door that we opened, and Grace and I both knew the moment we peeked inside that this was where

Morgan had been staying since he'd been released from prison. The place was in perfect order, everything put away properly, and the bed made with military precision.

"Wow, he was extremely neat, wasn't he?"

"I've heard that a lot of cons learn to be that way in prison and they are never able to break the habit once they are on the outside," I said. "At least it will make it easier to search, especially since Ellen knows what we're doing."

"Do you want the dresser, the closet, or that bag over there?"

"I'll take the dresser," I said as I pulled out the first drawer. Inside it, everything was neatly folded and in its proper place. I felt a bit of a twinge pawing through the dead man's things, no matter how badly he'd tried to treat my mother and me, but this search was vital to our investigation. "Remember, we're looking for an orange key, and anything else that might help."

"Do you have anything in particular in mind?"

"Evidence of who killed him would be nice, but if we can't find that, how about the items he used to blackmail everybody?"

"I'll give you a shout if I find anything," Grace said.

The top drawer was devoid of any clues, and I closed it and went on to the next in line. At this rate, we'd be done before Ellen got off for lunch.

I was finished with the bottom drawer without finding so much as a receipt when I decided to check the dust rail underneath it. I knew from personal experience that sometimes things could fall back behind a drawer. Who knew? Maybe I'd get lucky.

I didn't.

So far, my search had been a total waste of time.

I turned to Grace, who was just finishing up with the closet. "Did you find anything?" I asked her as I walked up to her.

"Not of consequence, and certainly no evidence, or any keys whatsoever."

"I guess that just leaves his bag," I said without too much conviction.

"You never know. He might have stuck something under his mattress. We might as well be thorough and check the bed while we're here."

"You take the bed, I'll grab the bag," I said as I looked at my watch. "We have about eight minutes, so we'd better get moving."

"I'm on it," Grace said as she started to tear up those beautifully crafted corners of the perfectly made bed.

While she did that, I started digging through the gym bag, hoping that something, anything, would turn up.

Thirty seconds later, I felt something in the lining, and after finding a hidden piece of Velcro sewn into the bag, I opened it and pulled out what we'd been looking for.

It was the orange key from the bus station!

Now we were getting somewhere.

"Grace, look what I found," I said as I held the key out to her.

"That's outstanding. I was just about to call for you. What do you think this means? I found it jammed behind the headboard."

She held up a piece of paper and waved it in the air. I took it from her as I handed her the key. As I studied the paper, I saw that it was a bank deposit slip. It was made out to a bank in Union Square, and the amount of the deposit was nine thousand eight hundred dollars.

It appeared that someone had actually paid Morgan off.

Had it been someone on our suspect list, or someone else entirely?

Only time would tell. We'd have to follow that lead as well, but at the moment, we had a locker to check.

My joy was tempered, though, when I heard a voice coming from the doorway.

"What did you find?" Ellen asked as she came into view.

Grace looked at me for a split second, and I nodded. I'd agreed to tell her everything. There was no going back on my word now. "It's the key to the bus station locker we've been looking all over for."

Ellen bit her lower lip, and then she said, "Let's go see what my brother was hiding, shall we?"

"We can take my Jeep," I said, but Ellen shook her head.

"I'll follow you in my car," she said as she held out her hand for the locker key.

"If you don't mind, we've been looking forward to opening it ourselves," I said. "We'd be happy for you to come with us, but we'd like to be the ones who open it."

After five seconds, Ellen answered, "Okay, I get that. I suppose you've earned at least that. Let me have my house keys back, and we're good to go."

As we drove to the station, Grace asked me, "Are we going to tell her about the deposit slip we found?"

"We're not at all sure what it means, or if we can even figure out who caved in," I said. "Why don't we hang onto it and see what we find in the locker? If it's holding what we think it is, then it's going to provide answers to some questions we don't even know enough to ask yet."

"I'm fine with it if you are," Grace said. "This isn't going to be all that pleasant for her, is it?"

"Confirmation that her brother really was blackmailing people? I can't see how it could be. She already knew that he was up to something, but this is going to be tough to take."

We all got to the bus station, and Grace pulled into an open spot. I wasn't all that surprised to see Ellen pull in right beside us. She'd been following close behind us during the entire drive over there. If we'd had any desire to get there early and sneak something out of the locker, she was going to make sure that didn't happen.

The three of us all walked in together, and my hand was shaking a little as I inserted the key and opened the locker.

We all looked inside at the same time, none of us sure what we might find, but I doubted that any of us would have guessed what was there.

There was nothing in the locker, not even a layer of dust. Whatever had been stored there before was now gone.

And we'd just run into another dead end.

"Well, that's that," Ellen said. Was there a hint of relief in her voice as she said it? "It was worth a shot."

"We're not going to give up just because *this* lead didn't work out," I said. "Your brother had to have done *something* with those files."

"You can keep looking all you want, but I'm finished," Ellen said. "This is all just taking too much out of me."

"What about those reports? Aren't you responsible for them?"

Ellen shrugged. "I already told my boss what I did. He reprimanded me and put something in my Personnel file, so as far as I'm concerned, it's over and done with. Good bye, ladies."

The police officer got into her car and drove away, and I realized that we hadn't mentioned the deposit slip we'd found. "Should we stop her and tell her about the slip?" I asked as I pulled it out of my pocket.

"Why would we? She just told us that she's done with the investigation. I don't feel as though we owe her anything at this point."

"Then what do we do with this?"

"Do we know anybody at this bank?" I asked.

"I don't know about you, but I don't."

"Then let's give it to Chief Martin," I said. "He's the only person we know who can walk into that bank and demand to see the records for Morgan Briar's account."

"Do you think he'll share what he finds out with us?" Grace asked.

"I hope so, but it doesn't really matter. One way or the other, *somebody* needs to look into this."

I called the chief of police, and I was a little surprised when I got him on the first try.

"Martin," he said.

"Chief, Grace and I were just at Ellen Briar's house, and we found something that you need to look into."

"I searched that room myself," the chief said unhappily. "Where did you find something? Hang on a second. How did you even *get* in there? Did you two actually break into a cop's house? Even I can't keep you out of jail if you did that."

"Don't be so quick to jump to conclusions," I said. "She gave us her keys."

That seemed to mollify him somewhat. "What did you find?"

"We found a deposit slip Morgan made out the day he was murdered," I said.

"I confiscated his checkbook," the chief said. "There was no record of a deposit that day."

"He probably just hadn't recorded it yet," I said. "Grace found it tucked away under the bed. It was stuck in the back of the headboard."

"And it just happened to *fall* back there?"

"From where she found it, it looked as though it was done on purpose," I said. "There's no way it could have just fallen back there by accident. Anybody could have missed it."

"You didn't. Where are you two now?" he asked.

"We're at the bus station in Union Square," I said.

"Planning on taking a trip, are you?" he asked with a hint of humor in his voice.

"No, it was just another lead that didn't pan out."

"Welcome to investigative work," he said. "I'm ten minutes away. Wait for me right where you are. I mean it, Suzanne. Don't go wandering off somewhere that I can't find you."

"We'll be here," I said.

Chief Martin was as good as his word, and we were both outside by the car waiting for him when he drove up and parked in the spot Ellen had so recently occupied.

"Let's see it," he said as he got out.

I held it back, though. "You should say please."

"Do you really want to push me on this? Okay, please."

"It's our pleasure," I said as I handed it over. "The bank's right across the street, if you want to check on it right now."

Chief Martin nodded, and then he started to cross the street.

Why was he the least bit surprised when Grace and I followed him?

The chief stopped dead in his tracks on the other side of the road. "Where do you two think that you are going?"

"Why, we just assumed that we'd go with you," Grace said.

"That's a dangerous assumption for you to make," he said. "This is part of my official investigation. There is no way that I can let you both just tag along."

"It was the 'please' crack I made, wasn't it?" I asked.

The chief let the hint of a smile escape before he reined it back in. "Just go back to your car and wait for me."

"And then you'll tell us what you found?" I asked.

"I'll think about it."

We really had no choice.

Grace and I crossed the street again and waited for the chief to return.

Chapter 16

Chief Martin came out of the bank ten minutes later, and I had a hunch that the branch manager had turned down his request. I was certain that a badge got him into many places that Grace and I couldn't reach, but I had a hunch they'd turned him down cold this time.

"They wouldn't tell you anything, would they?" I asked.

"What makes you think that?"

"I don't know. Am I right?"

"I got the information I was looking for, but I'm not at all sure that it's going to add anything to the case."

"How is that possible?" Grace asked. "What did they say?"

"The account was opened with cash," the chief said. "It was indeed done on the day of the murder, and the entire balance of the account was for one hundred dollars above the nine thousand eight hundred dollars."

"So then just one victim paid up," I said.

"That appears to be the case," the chief said. "We can't trace the cash, and it was just under the federal reporting limit, so there's nothing there, either. It's a dead end."

"I wouldn't say that," I spoke up. "If someone paid him, wouldn't that take them off our suspect list?"

"Maybe, maybe not. The victim may have felt remorse for caving in and then decided to track him down to kill him."

"He wouldn't have had the money *on* him," Grace said. "Morgan was many things, but he wasn't stupid."

"Then again, it might not have had anything to *do* with the money. Paying up meant giving up power, and somebody might not have been able to live with that."

"So then we all keep digging," I said.

"I can't endorse or condone that behavior," he said officiously, but then the police chief added almost under his breath, "Good luck."

"Thanks," I said just as softly.

After he was gone, Grace asked me, "Suzanne, is it my imagination, or is he softening up toward us?"

"I don't think it's in your head, though I have trouble believing it myself sometimes."

"Could his change of heart have anything to do with his relationship with your mother?" Grace asked me.

"Maybe a little, but I think it's more because he's seen what we can do. Our willingness to share information with him hasn't hurt, either."

"Whatever his reasons are, I'm glad that he's at least not trying to get us to quit anymore," Grace said.

"That makes two of us. Now, we've just managed to eliminate two clues that we thought might break this case wide open."

"Any thoughts about what we should do next?" she asked.

"I don't know about you, but I'm starving. I say we grab a bite to eat and then we go from there."

"Should we dare go back to Napoli's this soon?" Grace asked with a smile.

"Ordinarily I would be all for it, but I don't like eating there and not paying for my meal. It just goes against what I believe. There shouldn't be any free lunches."

"But sometimes you've been known to give donuts away," she reminded me.

"That's different," I said. After a moment's thought, I shrugged. "Okay, maybe it's *not* all that different. I don't know; I can't explain it."

"I'm not saying a word. Do you have any other ideas about where we can eat in Union Square besides Napoli's?" Grace asked.

"There's always Murphy's Diner," I said. I'd eaten there once when Napoli's had been closed for a family vacation, but truthfully, I hadn't been all that impressed with it.

"Didn't the health inspector close that place down?" Grace asked.

"No, not that I know of. Do you want to take a chance on it?"

"Not particularly," Grace said, "but I'm game if you are."

It wasn't an overwhelming endorsement, but it was the best that we could do on such short notice.

When we got there, there was a huge sign on the front door. It said,

"Closed For The Next Month While We Try To Make The Government Happy And Pass Their Stupid Inspection."

"Well, *that's* not good," I said as Grace pulled her car back out onto the street. "It looks like we're going to Napoli's after all."

As she started to drive, I noticed a beat-up old Ford truck again that I'd seen earlier. Was someone actually following us? "Grace, don't look now, but it seems that we've got a tail."

"Like in the movies?" she asked as she started to turn around.

I grabbed her shoulder. "I said don't look. Besides, you should be keeping your eyes on the road."

Of course she looked behind us, anyway. "You're not going to have *all* of the fun. Hey, I know that guy."

I tried to get another look behind us, but our attention must have warned him that we'd noticed him. The truck turned a hard left and disappeared from sight.

"Should I try to follow him?" Grace asked.

That's when I realized who had been driving that truck. "There's really no need to. It was Larry Landers."

"What's he doing following us around town?"

"I'm not sure, but I don't believe that it's a coincidence. Do you think it's possible that he killed Morgan, and now he's tailing us to get his hands on the blackmail evidence?"

"Is Larry really that bright?" Grace asked.

"I didn't say that he was smart, just that he could be greedy."

"It's possible. Whatever the reason, we need to keep an eye on him," she said.

"It might not be a bad thing to mention him to Chief Martin, and share the fact that he's following us around Union Square."

"We're out of his jurisdiction," Grace said, "but it wouldn't hurt. How are you going to handle our bill with Angelica?"

"I don't know. I was kind of hoping to just play it by ear."

"Oh, good. I can't wait to see this."

We found Angelica acting as hostess up front, something that she was doing more and more lately. As her three daughters became more adept in the kitchen, Angelica spent more time with her clientele. I wasn't sure whose idea it had been, but it seemed to work for them, not that I expected the switch to happen for the evening meal any time soon. Angelica was pretty possessive of her kitchen, even when her daughters were concerned.

"Ladies," she said with a broad smile. "I'm so happy that you decided to come back and visit us again so soon."

"We can't stay," I said, and I heard Grace take in a gulp of air beside me. Clearly my statement surprised her, and Angelica, too.

"And may I ask why not? Is our food no longer to your liking? I can assure you that my daughters are every bit as skilled in the kitchen as I am."

"Oh, we love your food," I said, "but if you're not going to let me pay for my meals, I'm sorry to say that I won't be coming back anytime soon."

Angelica frowned when she heard the news, and then she asked, "Are you willing to suffer the consequences of such a threat?"

I wasn't about to back down, though prudence told me that it wouldn't be a bad idea to do just that. "Angelica, you know me. Have you ever seen me walk away from a fight when I stated my position before?"

"No, I can't say that I have. Very well. You may pay." It was quite a concession on her part, and I was glad that she hadn't called my bluff. Not that I'd been bluffing. I'd meant every word I'd said, no matter how reluctant I would have been to follow through. Jake would have killed me, too. She did her best to put on a brave face as she led us inside. "If you'll follow me, I believe that I can find you a table."

We walked in behind her, and Angelica quietly seated us before disappearing into the kitchen.

"Wow, I thought you were about to blow that for good," Grace said.

"I wasn't sure myself, but I meant every word of it."

"I get that, but why didn't you tell her that *I* wouldn't mind if the free meals kept coming?"

I had to laugh, since Grace made five times what I brought home, and she could easily pay her bill even if she ordered the most expensive thing on the menu twice a day.

Sophia came out of the kitchen frowning, carrying a pair of menus. After she reached our table, she asked softly, "Suzanne, what did you just say to my mother?"

"Nothing," I said. "I just let her know that the free meals had to stop. Did she really take it that hard?" The idea of hurting my dear friend hadn't even entered my thoughts, and now I started to feel really bad about what I'd just said.

"Well, I've *never* seen her so subdued. I thought I would like it, but it's scaring everybody in the kitchen."

I had some fences to mend, and fast. "Bring her back out here, would you? I can't stand the thought that I hurt her feelings."

"Okay, but you should think hard about what you're going to do."

"Please, Sophia," I urged her.

"There are too many bosses around here these days," she said with a grin, but she did as I asked.

After a few moments, Angelica came back out into the dining room. "I understand that you wanted to see me?"

I stood up and hugged her, wrapping my arms around the woman I cared so much for. "Angelica, I was an idiot. Please find it in your heart to forgive me."

She stroked my hair for a few seconds, and then she pulled away. "There's nothing to forgive, Suzanne. Sometimes I get carried away. I give my food away as a way of saying I care. The last thing I wanted to do was to make you feel uncomfortable."

"I'm just too stubborn for my own good. If you still want to feed me for free today, I'll gladly accept it."

"Are you sure?" Angelica asked. "I don't want you to do anything you're uncomfortable with."

"I'm sure," I said.

"Hey, don't forget about me. I want to get in on this. *We're* sure," Grace said, correcting me.

It was a break in the tension that we all needed. Angelica laughed, showing her full range of good nature, as she said, "On one condition. I get to choose what you have."

I'd tried to fight my way through her never-ending meals before, but this was no time to try to draw a line in the sand. "That sounds great, but remember, we have more work to do today, so take it easy on us, okay?"

"No promises," Angelica said with a smile as she headed back to the kitchen.

Once the food started coming, I never thought it was going to end. By the end of the meal, Grace and I were sampling some Italian Ices, and I doubted I could get another bite down.

Angelica came over with a broad smile. "Did you two get enough to eat?"

"I'm not sure," Grace said. "Is there someplace I could take a nap and sleep some of this off?"

"If you're serious, you can use my office. I have an extremely comfortable couch in there."

"She'd love to," I said, "but unfortunately, I'm going to be keeping her busy. Angelica, may I ask you a question?"

"As long as it doesn't concern the bill, or even leaving a tip, you can ask me anything."

"Do you know a man in town named Fred Harmon?"

"Why are you looking for *him*?" she asked, her face

suddenly flooded with concern.

"Jake seems to think that he might be able to help us with the case we're working on," I admitted.

Angelica waved a hand in front of her. "Fred is quite harmless these days. I can't imagine him hurting a fly, let alone killing a man."

"This is about what happened to Blake Briar," I said.

Angelica nodded. "I always wondered about him." She took my hands in hers as she said, "I will tell you on one condition, but don't promise me if you can't do it. I couldn't stand seeing our friendship shattered over this."

"Does he really mean that much to you?"

"Not to me, but he once cared for someone very close to me. I need your word, Suzanne. If I tell you, you *have* to be gentle in your dealings with him."

"I promise that I'll do the best that I can," I said, knowing that Angelica never would have asked me for that kind of promise without having a good reason.

"Grace, the same goes for you."

She nodded. "You can count on both of us."

"Then I'll trust you both at your words. He's in the hospice over on Claremont Avenue."

"Is he dying?" I asked, wondering what was wrong with him.

"He's been fading away for a long time, but no one knows how much time that he has left. If you're serious about talking to him, I suggest that you do it as soon as possible."

"We'll leave right now," I said as I stood and hugged her. "The meal was exquisite. Thank you so much for your kind hospitality."

Grace added her own hug that echoed my sentiment.

"You are both such good girls," she said with a broad smile. "I'll call Fred and pave the way for you. Please, come again soon. Seeing you ladies does my heart good."

"You can count on it," I said as Grace nodded in agreement. "Your food is good enough to pay full price for."

When we walked into Fred Harmon's room at the hospice, I was afraid that we were too late. An emaciated man with thin, silver hair was sleeping there, swallowed up by the size of his bed. It was tough to see, and I didn't even know him. How much harder it must have been for those who cared about him, like Angelica.

Grace and I stepped back out of the room so that we wouldn't wake him, and I found a nurse with a nametag that said her name was Nancy nearby checking a chart.

"Excuse me," I said, "but we're here to see Mr. Harmon. Can he have visitors?"

The woman looked at us and smiled. "First of all, don't call him Mr. Harmon, at least not where he can hear you. It's Fred these days, and nothing else."

"Got it. Is he... okay?" I asked.

"No, I can't say that he is," the nurse said flatly.

"We can come back later," Grace offered.

"Hang on a second. Are you the girls Angelica DeAngelis called about?"

I grinned at her. "Neither one of us has been a girl in quite a while, but yes, she said that she'd call ahead to vouch for us."

"Honey, don't take it personally; she calls all of us girls. That's why we like it when she comes around. Well, that and the goodie bags she brings us. Fred asked me to wake him up when you got here. He desperately wants to speak to you. Come on back."

We followed her back into the room, and she gently touched Fred's shoulder when she reached his bed.

He came awake instantly, blinked a few times, and then he smiled at Nancy. "Hi there, beautiful," Fred said in a weakened voice.

"Listen to you," Nancy said gently. "You should know better than to flirt with me. I'm a happily married woman."

"Where there's life, there's hope," Fred said.

"Suzanne and Grace are here to see you," she said softly.

"Do I know them?" Fred asked, clearly puzzled to come

across our names.

"No, but Angelica sent them."

"Then they're okay by me," he said.

As we approached the bed, he asked, "Nancy, could we have a minute?"

"Are you sure you don't want me to hang around in case you need anything?" Nancy asked.

"Don't worry about me; I'm not ready to check out just yet."

"Well, don't do it without at least saying goodbye first," she said as she squeezed his hand.

After the pleasant nurse was gone, Fred said, "I don't know what I ever did to deserve her, but I'm not going to say it hasn't been welcome here in the end."

"What exactly is wrong with you?" Grace asked in her normal blunt fashion.

"That's none of our business," I said. Sometimes the gear between Grace's mouth and her brain got stuck in the open position, and I had to remind her to dial it back, especially after the promises we'd just made to Angelica.

"It's no secret," he said with the ghost of a smile. "It's my liver. Nobody can drink as much as I did and get away with it forever. The bill's been delivered, and I'm not far from paying it off in full."

"Did you know Blake Briar?" I asked. There was no easy way to pose the question, and none of us had time to beat around the bush.

"I knew him some, but mostly, I knew your father."

It was all I could do to keep from shouting. "How did you know him?"

"We were drinking buddies back in the bad old days," Fred said. "That man loved your mother more than anything in the world, and it killed him to be away from her."

"Why did he go, then?"

"In the end, it was nothing more than stubborn pride," Fred said, his voice still calm and level. "Jack was going through the darkest part of his days, and I was there to witness them firsthand myself, but he never wavered in his love for your mother."

"Tell us what happened," I asked, trying to match his soft tone. I didn't want to take the chance of upsetting a dying man, but I really did have to know. It was odd hearing my father called Jack and not Thomas, but at least that part of Morgan's story appeared to have been true.

Fred said, "I made a mistake, and then I did something even worse by trying to hide it. It's a long story though, and as I'm sure Nancy told you, I don't have a lot of time."

"Just hit the highlights, then," Grace suggested, matching our gentle tones of voice.

"I can do that. Jack, that's how he introduced himself back then, tried to bury his troubles in a bottle, and we happened to share the same kind of poison. You sit beside a man on the next barstool night after night, and you get to learn a lot about him—his history, his habits, even personal stuff he wouldn't tell his own mother. Anyway, we were drinking one night, and he kept passing out on me. Something was bothering him, but for once, I couldn't get it out of him. I finally grabbed his keys and drove him home, though I was not in much better shape than he was at the time. Somehow we made it back to his place, and I helped him into the room that he was renting. I realized when I got back outside that I had some use for his car myself, and I didn't have to think about it more than a second to borrow it without his permission."

Fred began to wheeze a little, and I was sure that he'd spoken more to us than he had in weeks. Nancy peeked in, but he waved her away, and she agreed with a silent nod, but not before giving us each a stern look.

"We can stop so that you can rest, if you need to," I said, but Fred wouldn't hear of it.

"I've been trying to get this off my chest for more years than I care to think about. It's about time to do it right now."

"Okay, but take your time. We're not in any hurry."

Fred smiled a little. "Maybe you're not, but I've got one

last ride to catch myself, and it won't be too far away. Back to what happened. I ran my errands, but instead of taking the car back to Jack's place, I stuck it in my garage. When I woke up the next morning, I'd forgotten all about having it. As a matter of fact, I didn't even think about it again until Jake told me that his car had been stolen. I didn't have the heart to tell him that I had it, and I planned to take it back to his place that night. I decided to turn in while I could still see the road, and I was on my way to his place when a squirrel jumped out in front of the car. At least I think it was a squirrel. It's been so many years, I'm not sure anymore if it was real or just in my imagination. I don't guess that it matters much now one way or the other. I jerked the wheel just as Blake was crossing the road. He never had a chance. I didn't even slow down, and I didn't stop until I was so far out of town that I was afraid I'd never make it back in time. I did, but just barely. When I got home, I turned on the radio and heard the bulletin that Blake was dead. I started to call the cops, and I would have told them everything if Jack had been arrested, but the police gave up pretty quick on that one. It turned out that I wasn't the only one drinking that night, and evidently Blake had quite a snootful himself. Whether it was my fault or not, I don't know to this day. Then, when Morgan was arrested for attacking Jack, I *couldn't* say anything. I was stuck, and there was nothing that I could do to make things right. If it matters," he asked, looking at both of us in turn, "I quit drinking. Oh, not right away, and never for very long, but my intentions were good, even if my spirit was weak."

Fred seemed to collapse back onto the bed, and Nancy came hurrying in. Before she could get rid of us, though, he said one last thing. "It was me all along. I'm sorry. I'm so sorry."

"You two need to leave," Nancy said sternly. "I hope your business with this man is done, because I don't think he could take it if you decided to come back."

I thought about telling Chief Martin what we'd just learned, if nothing else than to clear my father's name, but I couldn't do it to Fred, not and keep my word to Angelica. I'd tell Momma as soon as I got the chance, but it would be up to her to pursue it any further. I was pretty sure that I would tell Jake, but only if he promised not to do anything about it. I didn't have the heart to put this man through anything else.

It turned out that I needn't have worried about it, though.

Nancy caught us in the parking lot before we could even drive away.

"He passed away right after you left," she said. "I thought you should know."

"Did we kill him with our questioning?" I asked, mortified that I might have had a hand in killing this poor man.

"If you ask me, you did him a real service," Nancy said. "I knew that he was hanging onto what was left of his life because of some important unfinished business, but I had no idea that it would be with you. Telling you must have released him of whatever burden he unloaded onto you, and he just quietly slipped away. I swear, there was a smile on that man's face when he died that I *never* thought I'd see again."

"Thanks for telling us," I said as the tears started to flow unbidden down my cheeks.

Nancy touched my shoulder softly. "You have nothing to mourn, Suzanne. You honestly did him a favor by coming here today. Both of you did."

I just wished that I could find a way in my heart to believe that it was true.

LIGHT STICKS

No, these don't light up, but faces do when they taste them!
This is from another experiment I made looking through the
freezers in my grocery store. Again, these are simple to
make, but too delicious not to include. We like to eat these
while still warm, and spread our favorite jellies and jams on
top. They are impressive when you feed them to family and
friends, and they'll make you look like a real pro when you
put these out.

INGREDIENTS

Breadstick dough, 1 canister (I like the 11 oz. pack)
4 Tablespoons cinnamon sugar mix (3 Tablespoons
granulated sugar mixed with 3 teaspoons cinnamon)
 Assorted toppings of jams, jellies, butters, and spreads
Canola oil for frying (the amount depends on your pot or
fryer)

INSTRUCTIONS

Here's another recipe that's easy to make, yet impressive to
serve. Those are my favorites. If baking, see the directions
for the proper length of time and temperature (375 degrees F
for 10-12 minutes works for me). If you are frying, cook in
hot canola oil (360 to 370 degrees F) 1 1/2 to 3 minutes,
turning halfway through.
The breadsticks are segments, and I've tried twisting them in
the past, they mostly return to their straight form when
frying. I've added cinnamon sugar before frying, and then
dusted them again after they are finished!

Yield 12 Light Sticks

Chapter 17

"At least we know for sure that my father didn't kill anybody, accidentally or otherwise," I said as Grace and I drove back to April Springs. "I never really doubted it, but it was a relief hearing it straight from Fred."

"Are you going to tell your mother about what just happened?" Grace asked.

"Yes, and I'll tell Chief Martin now, too. He deserves to hear it, especially now that Fred is gone. As far as I'm concerned, he can do whatever he wants to with the information once we tell him."

We drove a little more in silence, and then Grace asked me, "I've been wondering where we should go from here."

"We just have to keep digging into Morgan's murder," I said.

"I realize that, but it all seems so overwhelming."

I considered it for a moment, and then I said, "Actually, our task just got a lot easier. Now that Blake Briar's death has been resolved, it's time to focus all of our energy on Morgan. He wasn't out of prison very long, but he surely managed to amass a group of people who wouldn't mind seeing him dead."

"You know, we never considered another possibility," Grace said. "What if somebody had a grudge against him in prison, and they decided to settle up once Morgan got out. He was always fighting when he was behind bars; that was what made his sentence run so long. Somebody that we've never even heard of could have taken the opportunity to get even with Morgan after he finally got out."

I just shrugged. "If that's the case, the *police* are going to have to solve his murder. They have access to a lot of information that we don't, like official records and the authority to ask questions that *have* to be answered. All we can do is poke and pry from the edges and hope we uncover something."

"Wow, it's tough being us sometimes," Grace said with a slight grin.

"Sure it is, but that's what makes it so much fun."

"Do you really call this fun?" she asked me.

"Hanging out with you and getting to stick my nose where it doesn't belong? How could that *not* be defined as fun?"

"I must be a little twisted," Grace said.

"Why's that?"

"Because I think that it's fun, too. If it weren't for the pesky occasional murder, it would be a blast. So, I ask again, what's next?"

"Do you have a pad and a pen in that bag of yours?"

"You know it," she said as she handed me her purse. "Just start digging. It's bound to be in there someplace."

I finally found what I was looking for, and as I pulled both items from her purse, I said, "Let's do what we do best and make a list of our suspects. At least this time we don't have to worry about motive. I've got a hunch that every one of them will be related to Morgan's blackmail scheme."

"Okay. I'm guessing we can leave you and your mother's name off this," Grace said.

"I've got a feeling that we're on enough other lists without adding our names here. We should start with Heather, Rose, and Martha Hickok."

As I finished writing, Grace said, "Whether we like it or not, we have to put Polly on it, too. And George."

I glanced over at her to see if she was serious. There was no smile on Grace's face. "Do you honestly think that *Polly* could have killed him? Or *George*? What would *his* motive be?"

"You know as well as I do how chivalrous that man is. If he thought Morgan was threatening his girlfriend, I could easily see him confronting the man, and then one thing could lead to another."

"I see the point that you're trying to make," I said. "But

murder?"

"I'm not saying that he did it on purpose, but he *has* a temper, and we both know it." She drove on a little longer, and then she added, "They both at least deserve a spot on our list."

"No," I said as I refused to write down either name. "If George did it, I'm not going to be the one who turns him in."

"I see that, but what about Polly?"

"I suppose that we have to add her name, but we can't tell George that we ever considered her a suspect. Agreed?"

"You bet. I don't want him mad at me any more than you do. That's still quite a list. Are we finished?"

"I'm going to put Larry Landers on it, too."

Grace looked over at me with a puzzled expression. "I thought that they were friends."

"Is there *really* honor among thieves, though? Larry could have found out about the blackmail scheme and then tried to cut himself in. I can't imagine Morgan standing for that, can you? It's not a stretch to think that they could have fought, and Morgan ended up dead. The only problem was that Larry didn't know where the evidence was hidden. That would explain why he's been following us around Union Square, too. He's hoping that we'll lead him to what he needs to continue blackmailing the victims."

"Okay, I see that. Is there anyone else we should add?"

"I don't know. Should Ellen's name be there, too?" I asked timidly.

"His *sister*? What would her motivation be?"

I thought about it. "I'm not really sure. It all hinges on whether she knew that he was blackmailing people with information from her files, or if she really just discovered it after we pointed it out to her."

"Maybe you should put her down, too, just so our list is as complete as we can make it. Should we add anyone else's name?"

I thought about the possibilities, and finally I shook my head. "That's it as far as I'm concerned. I'm not saying that the killer's name is definitively on our list, but if it's not, we don't have any hope of figuring out who did it."

As we pulled up into April Springs, Grace said, "I hate to bail on you, but I have a ton of paperwork that I've been putting off this week. Should we start fresh tomorrow after you close the donut shop?"

"Grace, you don't have to help me *every* day. I don't want you to get into trouble on my account; I know that you have a job to do."

"Suzanne Hart, there is no way that I'm letting you flush out a killer on your own. Don't worry about my job. I've got it all under control."

"If you say so," I said as she dropped me off.

My Jeep was still safely parked in our driveway, and Momma was there, too. I was glad about that. It would give me a chance to tell her Fred's story. Maybe it would bring a little peace into her life, and if I could that, I would do it gladly.

No mysteries tonight, though. Instead, she was doing a crossword puzzle when I walked in. "Suzanne, I didn't think I'd see you this evening. I'm waiting on Phillip to pick me up. We're going out."

"Salsa dancing?" I asked with a smile.

"Oh, yes. Care to tag along?"

"You're kidding, right?" I asked.

She smiled, and I felt the room brighten a little. "Of course I am. We're going to go see a movie. I meant what I said about joining us, though. You're welcome to come along, if you'd like."

It was a nice enough offer, but being the third wheel on one of my mother's dates was just about the last thing I wanted to do. "Thanks, but I've already seen it."

"I didn't tell you which movie we were seeing," Momma said.

"I know," I replied with a grin.

"Understood," she said.

"Momma, would you mind putting that down for a second? We need to talk."

She did as I asked, and then she asked, "It's never a good thing when someone says that, is it?"

"I think this time that it might be, actually."

"By all means, then, enlighten me."

I told her all I'd learned from Fred just before he died, and there were tears in Momma's eyes by the time I finished.

"Hey," I said as I touched her shoulder lightly. "This was supposed to be good news, remember?"

"Suzanne, I'm happy that this man confessed and cleared your father's name, but I can't help but mourn the time we lost together. I still miss him, and this case has brought back a flood of feelings I thought were long dead and buried. I hesitate to admit it since I don't want you to read too much into this, but this isn't the first time I've cried over Thomas in the past few days."

"It's only natural," I said. "Maybe now you can really let some of it go?"

She looked at me gravely as she spoke again. "I doubt that I'll *ever* be able to do that, but thank you for sharing this with me." Momma bit her lower lip, and then asked, "Does Phillip know?"

"I haven't told him yet," I said. "I thought I'd leave that up to you. Just say the word, and I'll call him right now."

"No, don't do that. I'll tell him when he comes to pick me up. It's not like Fred can be prosecuted for what happened at this point."

"I understand that," I said, "but it can't be an easy subject for you to discuss."

"Phillip and I are both adults. We can talk about this without getting emotional."

I whistled softly, and then I said, "Then you're both more grown up than I am. I couldn't do it."

"Don't discount how mature you've become, Suzanne. I hate to say it, but I think you've grown up quite a bit since your divorce."

"I kind of had to," I said. "Speaking of Max, have you heard the latest news about him?"

Her face clouded a bit. "Oh, dear. What's he done now?"

"It's not a bad thing. He's courting Emily Hargraves," I said. "If you can believe it, he even came by the donut shop and asked me for some advice about how to woo her."

"And you didn't hit him with a tray full of donuts? I'd say that you've learned to show remarkable restraint. What *did* you say to him when he asked?"

"I admit that, at first, I was going to blow him off, but the guy was so sincere, genuinely so, I ended up trying my best to help. Whatever he's doing must be working. I saw the two of them walking around town last night holding hands."

"My, my. It's a fascinating world we live in, isn't it?"

"It can be," I agreed when I heard a car pull up at the front. "That must be your date," I said as I stood.

"Let him come to the door," Momma said as she remained seated.

"You've really got him well trained, don't you?" I asked with a grin.

Her only response was a quick shake of her head, but I could swear that I saw a slight grin try to emerge before she managed to suppress it completely.

I gave her a quick hug, and then I headed upstairs. "If you don't mind, I don't particularly want to have a conversation with a police chief right now."

"Understood. There are leftovers in the fridge, and I made a fresh apple pie as well."

"You're too good to me. Have a good time tonight."

"I usually do," Momma said as there was a knock at the front door.

I didn't hang around long after that.

I was in my room before she opened the front door, and I watched from my bedroom window as they drove away.
Once I was sure they were gone, I walked back downstairs, grabbed a plate, a knife, and a fork, and I headed straight for the pie. That was my favorite order of eating, anyway. Why

would anyone in their right mind eat leftovers, even my mother's, when they could be having pie instead?

It was still hot the next morning as I made my way to Donut Hearts. I was beginning to wonder if this heat wave would ever end, and I found myself longing for cool weather again. As I drove up to the donut shop, I realized that the streetlight in front was burned out. Something about that gave me an uneasy feeling, and though I knew that I was probably just being paranoid, I drove past the shop, pulled into a parking spot down the block, and killed my headlights. Instead of getting out, though, I let my eyes adjust to the darkness first. Once I could see better, I scanned the area around Donut Hearts, searching for something, or perhaps *someone*, that didn't belong there. I waited at least ten minutes, and during the entire time, I didn't see anything move. Getting out of the Jeep, I closed my door as quietly as I could, and then headed back up the street toward my donut shop.

I was nearly there when I felt glass crack under my shoes. Looking around on the ground, I realized that there were shattered pieces everywhere.

The light hadn't burned out after all.

Someone had destroyed it, and I had a very bad feeling about who might have done it.

Without giving it another thought, I started hurrying back to my Jeep as I reached for my phone to dial 911.

I never made it, though.

Stepping out of the shadows, someone grabbed my arm, and my cell phone clattered to the ground.

"What do you want, Larry?" I asked as I made out my assailant. It was Morgan's best friend, Larry Landers, and he didn't look happy at all.

"Where is it, Suzanne? I know you know, so don't try to play dumb with me."

"Who's *playing*?" I asked. "I don't have any idea what

you're talking about. Let me go, Larry."

I'd tried to use my most authoritative voice, but he didn't respond to my command. Instead, he tightened his grip even harder. "That hurts," I said.

"It's about to hurt a lot worse if you don't tell me the truth. I want that blackmail information, and I want it now."

"We haven't found it yet," I said.

"Why should I believe you?"

"You were following us around all day yesterday. Did it *look* like we found anything?"

I could make out a frown on his face in the near darkness. Maybe I should have lied to him. I couldn't be in a worse position than I was at the moment, and at least I might have been able to buy myself some time. "You *knew* that I was watching, so you didn't want to tip your hand. I can't trust anything you tell me, can I? I hate that it's come to this, but if I can't believe that you're telling me the truth, why do I even need you anymore?"

He drew back his free hand, and I readied myself for the blow that I knew was about to land.

And then, in an instant, a light blinded us both, and Larry's grip eased as a voice near the light commanded, "Hit the ground and put your hands behind your head."

Larry disobeyed, whether he was frozen in the moment, or he chose not to move for some other reason, and the voice ordered, "This is your last warning. If you do not immediately comply, I *will* shoot you."

"Do what he says," I pled with Larry. It wasn't that I cared so much about him; I just didn't want to see him shot dead while I was standing right beside him.

My words seemed to have some impact on him, because Larry finally released me and dropped to the ground. I took a step backward, and an instant later Chief Martin was on top of him, cuffing him, and then pulling him up to his feet in easy, practiced motions. The chief must have been pumped up on adrenaline, because he had no problem at all doing it, even though Larry was no small man.

"Are you all right?" Chief Martin asked me as he steered Larry toward his squad car.

"I'm fine," I said, even though my voice was a little bit shaky. I would probably get a bruise on my arm from the way Larry had grabbed me, but it could have been worse—a lot worse.

I started to walk back to the donut shop when the chief called out, "Are you really going to open up the donut shop after what just happened?"

"My customers are depending on me," I said. What I didn't tell him was that I needed the comfort and assurance of that part of my life to help me cope with what just happened.

"I can understand that. At least you don't have to worry about the murderer coming after you anymore," the chief said.

That got Larry's attention. "Are you talking about me? I didn't kill anybody!"

"Yeah, and we should believe you *why*, exactly?" Chief Martin asked. "Because otherwise, you're a respectable kind of guy?"

"I might have wanted to take over his blackmail business, but I never would have laid a hand on Morgan. He was the only friend I had in the world. I never would have killed him."

"Shut up and get in the car."

"I didn't kill him," Larry repeated.

The chief shook his head, and then he shrugged. "We heard you the first time."

Once they were both gone, I unlocked the front door of the donut shop, flipped on the outside lights, and then I got out my broom and dustpan. I couldn't have my customers walking across glass to get to me, and I felt better taking care of that first.

When the sidewalk was clean, I went back inside and started my daily routine as though nothing had happened. Getting my hands into the flour, sugar, butter, and yeast was just what I needed, and I could feel my stress start to vanish as I converted the raw ingredients into dough.

Chapter 18

"The streetlight's out in front," Emma said casually as she walked back into the kitchen as her shift started. "You might want to get someone to take a look at that."

"Thanks. I already made the call," I said. "By the way, it didn't burn out. Somebody broke it on purpose."

"What's wrong with people these days? Don't they respect anything anymore? Sometimes it just drives me nuts with the random vandalism we're seeing."

"I didn't realize that you felt that strongly about it."

"Dad just wrote an editorial about it, and he got me all fired up. Sorry about that."

"That's okay. Actually, there wasn't anything random about this. Someone did it so they could catch me by surprise."

"Seriously?" Emma asked. "Who would do that to you? You weren't hurt, were you?"

I rubbed my arm where Larry had grabbed me, and I could feel how tender it was. "No, not much, anyway."

"Who did it? Did they get away?"

"No. He's in jail right now, as a matter of fact. As much as I like to complain about Chief Martin, he really saved me this morning." I brought her up to date about Larry Landers and his attack, but I didn't mention anything about his close ties to Morgan Briar, or the blackmailing scheme he'd been trying to take over.

Emma frowned when she heard the news, bit her lip for half a second, and then she shook her head. I knew exactly what she was thinking. She wanted to call her father and report what had happened to me, but we'd had words about that behavior before, so I knew that she was reticent to push me too far.

"Go on. Call him," I said. She might as well be the one who offered him the tip. Her dad would find out himself soon enough when he read the police arrest blotter.

Emma looked down at the floor. "Nope. I'm not going to do it this time."

"I'm giving you my blessing. Call him before someone else does. At least that way you'll get his crimestopper's tip money."

"Okay. If you're sure."

"I'm sure. You'd better hurry up and do it, or I might just be tempted to call it in myself." I tried my best to smile as I said it, but I wasn't sure that I was convincing at all.

Emma grabbed her phone, and I kept working on the dough for the day's cake donuts. She came back in just as I started to drop donuts, so I shooed her right back out again. I'd let the dropper slip out of my hands once, and I wasn't about to let anyone near me again while I was working with it.

When I called for her to come back in, she was smiling.

"I take it that your father was happy to get the tip," I asked.

"You might say that. He told me to tell you that he'd pay you twice what I just got if you'd give him an exclusive interview about the attack."

I had to laugh. "Do you even have to ask for my answer?"

"Just tell him that I pitched the idea to you, okay?"

"Sure thing," I said. "I can do that."

"It's funny, but Dad was in such a good mood that he volunteered to share some information about the case you've been working on."

"Why does he think that I'm doing anything?" I asked. If Chief Martin was right, the case had just ended with Larry Landers's arrest.

"Come on. He *knows* what you and Grace have been up to. So, do you want it, or not?"

"Why not? What did he have to say?"

"It seems that Martha Hickok has been going around town bragging about someone trying to blackmail her with risqué photographs."

"I thought that she was trying to keep that a secret," I said as I remembered her clandestine conversation with Jake about it.

"Apparently she changed her mind. Dad said that he wondered if she told him about it so she could take out a front page ad, but it turns out that instead, it ended up giving her an alibi by accident."

"Why is that?" I asked, curious about what Martha had been up to.

"It turns out that she was playing Midnight Bingo in Hickory when Morgan was murdered," Emma said. "Evidently, the first game starts at nine and they finish up around one a.m., so she was too far away to get back in time."

"She could have always slipped out, and then come back again," I said, though I had a hard time envisioning Martha as a murderer.

"The tickets are time-stamped, and once you leave, you can't get back in. That's not the kicker, though. Martha doesn't drive, so she couldn't have done it. She rode the bus down, and then she rode it back when the last game was over."

I took all of that in, and then I nodded. It worked for me. "Tell your dad that I said thanks, and that I owe him one."

"Enough to do the interview he wants to do with you?" Emma asked with a smile.

"Not quite," I replied, happy that I'd at least managed to strike *someone* else's name off my list, no matter how little the viability of the candidate was. If I discounted Larry as the murderer, that just left Rose, Heather, Cliff, and Polly. George might still be a remote suspect, and so was Ellen for that matter, but I had a feeling that one of them was a murderer. Now all I had to do was figure out which one was guilty, and that wasn't going to be easy.

"Suzanne, are you all right?" Momma asked me half an hour after Chief Martin had left the scene with Larry Landers.

"I'm fine. What are you doing up so early?"

"Phillip called me, of course," she said. "Is it true? Did he catch the killer?"

"I don't think so," I said.

After a moment's pause, Momma said, "Then I'm confused. Phillip is under the impression that this Landers man killed Morgan Briar."

"He might be positive, but I'm still not convinced," I said.

"What makes you think that he's *not* the one?"

"I can't say for sure," I admitted, "but I just don't believe it."

Momma sighed, and then she said, "Well, I've grown to trust your instincts over the years. Be careful."

"I always am," I said. "Now why don't you go back to sleep?"

"So you can get back to your donut-making?" she asked.

"I can't fool you, can I?"

After I hung up, I told Emma, "That was my mother. She was worried about me."

"Do they ever stop?" Emma asked.

"Not as far as I can tell. Sometimes I fuss about her being a little too overprotective with me, but in the end, it's nice to have someone who worries about me."

"I'm sure Jake does, too. When are you going to tell him what happened?"

I shook my head. "I'm not, at least not until I'm satisfied that this case is over. All it would accomplish would be to cause him needless worry, and he has enough to focus on with what he's doing."

"Are you sure? He might be upset if he finds out that you held something back from him," Emma said.

"Maybe, but he knows me well enough to realize that I have reasons for the things I do. Now, would you grab more vanilla extract from the storage room?"

"I'd be happy to," she said. As Emma left the kitchen, I thought about calling Jake, but he was most likely still asleep, and I didn't feel right waking him. That was only part of it, though. What I'd told Emma was the truth. There was nothing that he could do about what had happened earlier, and the last thing I wanted was for him to rush back to April Springs because I couldn't take care of myself. If I truly believed that I needed him, I'd call him in a heartbeat, but for now, I'd save that phone call for later.

In the meantime, I had donuts to make.

I'd been open ten minutes when Chief Martin pulled up outside in his squad car. Since he'd started dating Momma, he'd stopped eating donuts in an effort to lose weight, and he'd been quite successful at it. The man was practically wasting away, but I still couldn't entice him with one of my treats.

Before he could get in the door, I poured him a cup of coffee and had it waiting for him. "Care for some coffee?" I asked as he walked in.

"That would be great. I haven't been to bed yet."

"You never told me how you happened to be there when I needed you. Not that I'm not grateful, but it was a pretty big coincidence."

"It wasn't a coincidence at all," he admitted. "I was working on something else, and I thought I'd swing by the donut shop to check up on you on my way home."

"Were you spying on me, Chief?" I asked him with a grin. "Don't tell me that my mother put you up to it."

"She's worried about you, and if I can help ease some of her fears without costing me too much more than a little sleep, why wouldn't I? Do you really mind all that much?"

I kissed him on the cheek, something that made him blush instantly, and I said, "No, I want to thank you for it. As much as I like to believe that I'm a modern woman capable of handling any situation, I appreciated the fact that you were there when I needed you more than I can say."

He looked absolutely flabbergasted by my compliment, which made me smile broadly.

"Uh, I was happy to do it," he said as he tried, and failed, to make eye contact with me. After another sip of coffee, the police chief added, "Your mother is still worried about you, you know. She told me that you're still not convinced that Larry Landers killed Morgan Briar."

"I'm not," I said. "When did she tell you that?"

"Right after the two of you spoke," he said. "Listen, I know how these things can be, but you don't have anything to worry about. The case is over."

"I just don't buy it," I said. "There's no evidence that Larry killed Morgan, and besides, there are a ton of other people who had more of a motive than just greed."

"Don't sell avarice short," the chief said. "You'd be amazed by how many people commit the most horrific acts just because they want something that someone else has."

"I realize that, but fear is an even bigger motivator, wouldn't you say? Someone you'd never dream of as being capable of killing could commit murder if they were backed into a corner." Jake had told me that enough times that I had no doubt that it was true.

"I understand that, but it's not the case this time."

"Convince me," I said.

He thought about it for a few seconds, and then he said, "Tell me the names of your other suspects, one at a time, and I'll do the best that I can do."

I considered his offer, and then I nodded. "You've got yourself a deal. Let's start with the blackmail victims themselves. First up, we have Heather Morningstar, and her fiancé, Cliff."

"They had dinner in Charlotte the night of the murder, and then they went to a formal ball. Half a dozen witnesses verified that, so they're both in clear."

"It would have been nice knowing that earlier," I said with a frown.

"Young lady, you are *not* privy to what my department knows. I'm doing this strictly as a courtesy, so don't give me a reason to walk out of here. If I do, your mother won't be pleased with either one of us."

"Sorry," I said, promising myself to put my petulance

aside. "How about the florist in Union Square named Rose? I don't know her last name."

Without even consulting his notes, he said, "She was in the Emergency Room with her mother. We've got video surveillance that proves it."

Suspects were falling like snowflakes, and I had to wonder if the chief might be right after all. He asked, "Who else is on your list?"

I didn't want to admit it to him, but I didn't really have any choice. "I know that it sounds crazy, but Polly North had a motive, and if she told George, he has to be on the list, too."

"Let me get this straight. Are you accusing your friend, and our mayor, of murder?"

"Of course not," I said. "I just couldn't mark them off my list without a better reason than because I like them. Do you have alibis for them?"

"If you want to go grill them, feel free, but I'm satisfied that I have the right man. Is there," he started to say as his radio called him. "Hang on. I have to answer this." After a whispered conversation, the chief turned to me and said, "I've got to go. Somebody just ran a stoplight and plowed into a motorcycle."

"How bad is it?" I asked.

"Sounds like it's bad enough. Thanks for the coffee," he said as he shoved the mug into my hands and left, his siren wailing and his lights flashing as he tore up the road.

Emma heard it, even through her earbuds, which were now dangling down onto her shoulders. "What was that all about?"

"The chief came by, but there was an emergency situation that he had to deal with, so he had to go."

Emma nodded, put the buds back in, and then she went back into the kitchen. As I rinsed the mug and put it into one of the plastic tubs we used to collect dirty dishes, I had to wonder if Chief Martin was right. Could Larry Landers be the killer after all? Was I reluctant to accept that, since I hadn't been the one who'd discovered his guilt? I had to admit that it was possible that it was my ego, and not the facts, that was holding me back. I'd have to discuss it with Grace when she came in later, but for now, it was time to run my donut shop.

The morning seemed to drag on forever, and I cursed the rising temperature yet again. I had the air conditioner cranked up to its highest setting, but it still had a hard time keeping up with the heat that shot in whenever someone opened the door. Finally, at a quarter until eleven, I walked back to where Emma was sitting at her workstation, and I found her with her nose buried in a textbook.

My assistant looked startled to find me suddenly standing in front of her, and she quickly pulled out her earbuds. "Sorry. I got caught up on my work, so I thought I'd prep for a test I've got later this afternoon."

"I'm just happy that you found something productive to do," I admitted. "I finished the crossword puzzle and started working on the number puzzle in the newspaper."

"Are you having any luck?" she asked.

"No, my mind just doesn't work that way. I'm more of a word kind of gal." I looked around, and the kitchen was indeed spotless. "Why don't you go ahead and take off?"

"Are you sure? I'd be glad to hang around until we close."

"We officially are," I said. "I'll walk you out, and then I'm locking up early."

"Sold," she said. "I need the time off to study more than I need the money."

"Well," I said with a grin, "you're going to get both. I'll pay you for the end of your shift. Good luck on that exam."

"Thanks," she said as she scooted out the door. I was about to flip the OPEN sign to CLOSED when a strange woman came rushing toward me.

I held the door for her, and as she came in, she scolded me. "You're supposed to be open until eleven."

"Things were a little slow, so I decided to close early."

She looked disappointed as she started to walk out again. I said quickly, "I'll be glad to wait on you, though."

"Really?" she asked.

"Really. What can I get you?"

She looked at each of the display cases, and then, without a moment's hesitation, she said, "I'll take it all."

"*All* of it?" I asked. There were five dozen assorted donuts left, as well as thirty or forty donut holes.

"The whole lot. My husband just got out of the hospital, and he kept saying the entire time that he was in there that all he wanted in the world was your donuts. Do you know Greg Whitmore? He's tall and lanky, and has the cutest blue eyes you've ever seen."

"Sure, I know your husband. Greg's a good customer," I said. "I was wondering why I hadn't seen him around lately. How's he doing?"

"Pretty good now, but it was touch and go for a while."

"What happened to him, if you don't mind me asking?"

She looked as though she wanted to cry as she said, "He was in a car wreck on his way to the beach to spend the weekend with me. I was down there for a conference, and he was coming down to surprise me."

"I'm glad that he's going to be okay. You know, he usually just gets a couple of glazed donuts and a black coffee. Are you sure you want everything?"

She grinned at me as she said, "I want it all."

"Okay, then." I boxed everything up, and then I handed the stack to her.

"What do I owe you?" she asked as she started to dig out her wallet.

"They're on the house," I said. "Tell him that I hope he's back here himself soon."

"He told me what a great woman you were," she said. "But if I don't pay for these, he'll be very unhappy with me, and I don't want to stress him out any. Will you *please* take my money?"

It wasn't often that someone begged to pay me for my

donuts. "As a favor to you, I will. How does ten dollars sound?"

"These donuts are worth a lot more than that to me. How about forty?"

"I'll take twenty, and that's my final offer," I said with a smile.

She returned it, and then she put the bill on the counter. "Sold. Could you get the door for me? I'm parked just over there."

"I'll do better than that," I said. "You get the door, and I'll carry them to the car *for* you."

"You don't have to do that."

"I know, but I want to. It's just part of the Donut Hearts service."

After we had them loaded up, Greg's wife surprised me by hugging me. "Thank you so much, Suzanne. I'm so happy that he's coming home, I just about can't stand it."

"I'm happy for both of you," I said, and then I watched her get into her car and drive away.

Walking back to the shop, I spotted Max strolling down the sidewalk toward me.

"How's it going?" I asked. "I saw you out walking with Emily."

He grinned at me, showing his perfect teeth. "It's all a part of our courtship. She told me that we had to take this slow, the old-fashioned way, so I'm doing my best to woo her. Can you believe that?"

"Max, I'm actually proud of you," I said. "I sincerely hope that it works out. Just be careful. If you break her heart, you might have to leave town for good. Folks around here really love that woman and her three stuffed animals."

"You don't have to tell me," Max said. "She's working on new costumes for them right now."

"Care to share any hints with me?" I asked.

"I'm not supposed to," he replied.

"That's fine. I understand."

Max looked up and down the street to confirm that we

were alone, and then he said softly, "You know what? I trust you. She's dressing Spots and Cow up as two moose, and Moose is going to wear a cow outfit. It's pretty cool, actually."

"I'm glad that you're getting along," I said.

"So far, so good, and I owe a great deal of it to you."

"Don't give me *too* much credit," I said. "You're the one doing the work."

"It's not work if you love doing it," he replied with a grin. "I won't forget that you're the one who got her to agree to give me another chance."

"I'm glad you're making the most of it."

I headed back to the shop and finished cleaning up, something that was much easier now that I was sold out of donuts. I was just filling out my deposit slip, as meager as it was, when Grace tapped on the front door.

It looked as though she was ready to start investigating again with me, but I wasn't sure how happy she'd be about it when she read the last few names that were left on our list. The only legitimate suspects we still had besides the man now in jail were two good friends of ours. I'd discounted Ellen, feeling as though she wouldn't kill her last surviving brother under any circumstances. It had been crazy to include her name in the first place, almost as insane as it was to add Polly and George. A part of me wanted to just let everything go and trust Chief Martin when he said that he'd solved the case, since my true list of viable suspects was probably worthless. After all, he got *paid* to find the bad guys, while Grace and I were amateurs at it, no matter what our success rate had been in the past. Even Jake had open cases on his desk, crimes that he'd been unable to solve over the years for one reason or another. How arrogant was it of Grace and me to believe that *we* had to be the ones who caught up with every culprit? If I knew what was good for me, I'd let this go and move on with my life.

If only I could find a way to shut up that nagging suspicion in the back of my mind that the killer was still somewhere out there.

Chapter 19

After I brought Grace up to date on what Chief Martin had told me, she looked as deflated as I'd felt hearing that nearly all of our suspects had alibis for the murder.

"Where does that leave us?" she asked.

"In reality, the only ones left who *need* alibis are Polly and George."

"Why didn't Chief Martin ask them for theirs?" Grace asked.

"George is his boss. Unless he has a better reason to suspect him that he does right now, it's a delicate issue to dance around."

"Well, he's our *friend*. How much more delicate is that? You realize that he's not going to like the questions that we have to ask him, don't you?"

"I'm beginning to wonder if we should just do what everybody keeps telling us and drop this entirely. Chief Martin is so sure that he's got the right man for it. What if we alienate George and Polly for nothing? I couldn't stand to hurt those friendships, could you?"

"No, they both mean a lot to me as well. Is there any way to ask George for an alibi *without* arousing his suspicions?"

I thought about it, and then I shook my head. "The man has better instincts than most cops still working the job. He'll know what we're doing before we even get the chance to open our mouths. I can't see any way possible that subterfuge could work, and in many ways, Polly is just as sharp as he is. I keep thinking that this crime is too *ordinary* for either one of them to have committed it. Does that make any sense at all?"

"It might, if we thought that it had been premeditated, but from what Chief Martin told us, it looked like a simple assault gone bad. With George's temper, I'm afraid that it fits the pattern all too well. I don't guess we have any real choice, do we?"

"We might as well go ahead and get it over with," I said as I shook the keys to my Jeep.

"You're right. Well, it was nice knowing you," Grace said.

"I second that, but maybe we'll figure out a way to survive this before we get over there."

Grace pointed to the building where George's office was located. "I don't see how. Should we drive around some first before we tackle them?"

"Are you suggesting that we stall?" I asked her.

"Absolutely one hundred percent," she replied.

I thought about it, and I realized that most likely, delaying the inevitable would do us no good at all. Then again, it did postpone our pain, and at the moment, I was all for anything that could do that. "Why don't we drive over to Union Square? Maybe there's something there that we missed?"

"It's worth a shot," Grace said. "And if nothing else, it buys us at least an hour before we have to go talk to George."

I knew it was foolish to delay the conversation that we needed to have, but I didn't care. The air conditioner in my Jeep wasn't much, though. "Maybe we should take your company car instead," I suggested.

"Why? Do you feel like riding around in style for a change of pace?"

"Actually, it's your air conditioning that I covet. My Jeep's great for most kinds of weather, but it's not exactly suited for this heat we're having."

"That makes sense to me," Grace said. "I'd be happy to drive."

As we headed out of town, I asked my best friend, "Are we wrong in pursuing this? Could Larry Landers really have killed Morgan Briar?"

"I guess that it's possible, but if he did, why would he wait to do it in April Springs?" Grace asked.

"It could be that he wanted to divert suspicion onto our town instead of his," I said. "If Morgan were killed in Union

Square, we might have a totally different list of suspects."

"That's true," Grace said.

She added something else, but it was lost on me. I'd never considered the possibility before, but it kept echoing over and over in my mind. How would we have handled things differently if Morgan had been murdered in Union Square? The first thing we would have done would be to look at the suspects *there* a little harder. But planning it that way would take a pretty cunning mind, and none of his victims that we knew of could ever be accused of being master criminals. Which one might know enough about how the police investigate a crime to intentionally try to lead everyone digging into the murder astray?

And when I looked at it that way, only one name came to mind.

The only problem was that neither Grace nor I had a shred of evidence that might prove that I might be right.

At least not yet.

"I think I know who did it," I said so softly that Grace nearly missed it.

"Come again?" she asked.

"I believe that Ellen Briar killed her brother."

"I know you're not talking about Blake. We've already heard *that* confession. Why should she kill Morgan?"

"Her reputation as a police officer means *everything* to her," I said. "She told us herself that she was trying to make detective and get back on the street. How was her boss going to take it when he found out that she had a blackmailer living under the same roof as she was?"

"She already told him, though, remember?" Grace reminded me.

"No, she told *us* that she confessed everything to him, but how do we know that she *really* did it? We just can't ask her boss straight out."

"Maybe we can't, but someone else could."

Grace shook her head as she asked, "You're not seriously

going to ask Chief Martin to check for you, are you?"

"I don't have much choice," I said as I reached for my phone. "Jake's out of touch, and there's no one else that I can turn to."

"Good luck with that," Grace said as I dialed the chief's number. "Hang on a second. Before you call Chief Martin, answer me this. Why would Ellen *ever* let us search Morgan's room if she were the one who killed him? We found the key there, but the locker at the bus station was already empty, remember?"

"What if she cleaned it out, and then she invited *us* over to find the key ourselves so that we'd drop our investigation?" I asked.

"I can see that. Go on, make your telephone call."

It wasn't something I particularly wanted to do, but if I could prove that Ellen had lied to us, it might just be a crack that we could use to break the case wide open.

"No."

"You won't even try?" I asked the chief after he flatly refused my request.

"That is correct. You've lost your mind even asking me to do this, Suzanne. I'm going to do you a favor and forget that we ever *had* this conversation."

"But what if she's the one who killed her brother?" I asked.

"Go home, Suzanne."

I was about to reply when I realized that he'd already hung up on me.

"No luck, huh?" Grace asked as I put my phone back in my pocket.

"No, but I'm not willing to give up that easily. There's got to be something else that we can do." After a moment, I added, "I've got it. We'll just have to break into Ellen's place and see if we can find *anything* that points to her as the killer."

Grace looked over at me as though I'd just lost my mind.

"Suzanne, even if I accept your premise, which I don't, at least not one hundred percent, do you realize what you're planning to do is insane? What if we get caught? That's going to be a jam that nobody's going to be able to get us out of, not even Jake. He already told you that himself, remember? When you suggested we break into Ellen Briar's place before, I never really took you seriously, but this time, it's *exactly* what you want us to do, isn't it?"

"Is it really breaking and entering if we steal her keys at the police station?"

"Yes!" she said loudly.

"Does that mean that you don't want to do it with me?"

Grace seemed to think about that, and then she shrugged. "No, I'll go along with you. After all, you're going to need a friendly face in prison when we both get put away. I just hope they keep us together."

"It won't hurt to ask," I said as I headed over to the police station.

It was time for a desperate act that might just catch a killer.

"What are you two doing here?" Ellen was surprised to see us; that much was clear.

"We need to talk to you outside," I said, nearly out of breath. "I wouldn't ask if it weren't important." Grace and I had jogged in place outside for a few minutes before we went in. We had a plan, and it depended on Ellen buying our setup if we were going to have any chance of getting her keys without her knowing it.

"I'm on the desk," she said. "What is it?"

"We found a guy who saw Morgan just before he was murdered. He thinks that he might be able to identify the killer."

A flicker of alarm crossed her face, and she barked out to Denise, the young woman who'd been vying to replace her, "Take the front."

Ellen headed for the front door, and it was time to put our

plan into action. I stumbled against her as she went through
the threshold, knocking her into Grace. As we untangled
ourselves, I took the keys I'd slipped off her belt and put them
in my pocket.

It had worked.

Or had it?

"Hang on. Something's wrong," Ellen said.

Had we been caught in the act? "What is it?" I asked as I
put a hand back on the keys. I'd be ready to drop them at a
moment's notice and claim they'd come off her belt in the
collision.

She looked outside instead, though. "Where's your
witness?"

"He must have run off," I said.

"Well, find him," she barked out.

After we conducted a ten-minute search for someone who
was a figment of my imagination, I said, "It's no good. He's
gone."

"Did you at least get his name?" Ellen asked with
irritation.

"Of course we did. It was Jack Smith."

"Jack, as in John? Seriously? What did the guy look
like?"

"He was kind of average," Grace said. "We can find him
again. I'm sure of it."

"When you do," she said, "call me. Don't tell anyone
else. I want to handle this myself. I deserve to be the one
who tracks down my brother's killer."

"We promise," I said as we walked back to the station,
praying that she didn't realize that her keys were gone.

After we split up, Grace looked at me anxiously. "Did
you get them?"

"It worked perfectly. Let's go have another look around
that house."

"You're some kind of criminal genius," she said with a
grin. "Maybe you're working for the wrong team."

"I'm happy being one of the good guys," I said as we

headed for her car. "I don't know how much time we've got, though, so we'd better hurry."

I fumbled the keys a little at the door as Grace stood impatiently behind me. "Do you want me to try it?"

"I've got it!" I snapped, and then the right key slid into place.

"Sorry," Grace said as she looked around behind us. "I guess I'm just a little paranoid."

"I should be the one apologizing. I shouldn't have yelled at you," I said as the door opened.

"Where do we look first?"

"If there's anything here to find, it's got to be in that file cabinet," I said as I hurried to the cabinet. I found the right key immediately, and as Grace and I searched the files, I was almost relieved when I found the police report she had filed about Polly. If it had ever been stolen, it was back in its proper place now.

That's when I realized that my hunch had been on the money. Ellen had found at least some of the files herself, and instead of turning them in to the police chief, she'd slipped them back into her files. That made her look guilty, or at the very least, culpable in some way.

None of the files for our other suspects were there, though.

"I'm not sure *what* to do now," I said as I closed the last drawer. "Should we search the place again?"

"Suzanne, we found *one* file," Grace said. "That's *got* to be enough proof that she's involved in her brother's murder."

"It won't work," I said. "She could have made a duplicate file. Or at the very least, she could lie about it and say that she did. If it's her word against ours, who is anyone going to believe? We've got to find something else."

"There's no time," Grace said as she touched my arm. "Ellen could realize that her keys are gone at any second. If she catches us here, we're dead, and I mean that literally. We need to come up with another plan later, but right now, we need to go."

I knew that she was right, but I didn't have to like it.

"Come on," Grace said as she pulled me out the door. I quickly locked it behind us, and then I asked her, "How are we going to get Ellen's keys back to her without her realizing that we stole them in the first place?"

"We'll just drop them on the sidewalk in front of the police station," I said. "Somebody will surely turn them in."

"That sounds good," Grace said. "Let's get out of here."

I started to follow her as I walked past the doghouse, touching the roof again lightly as I went past it.

And then I stopped dead in my tracks.

Grace looked back at me, clearly puzzled by my hesitation. "We have to *go*, Suzanne."

"Not just yet," I said. "Do you remember that I told you that Ellen said she was allergic to just about everything?"

"Sure, I remember."

"Well, one of the things that she mentioned was that she was allergic to dogs. The question is, why does she have a doghouse on her property, and even more, why is it freshly painted?"

"I don't know," Grace said as some of her frustration came out. "Maybe there never was a dog, and she's just using it as a yard decoration."

"Or maybe it's something more. Morgan could have done this himself."

"Fine, Morgan did it. Does it really matter?"

"It might," I said as I got down on my hands and knees and started to poke my head inside.

"Are you serious?"

"It'll just take a second." I couldn't see anything on the ground, but then I looked up. There was new wood there, something built like a shelf. Could it be important?

As I was reaching for it, Grace asked me, "Suzanne, why does this matter?"

"Because I just found this," I said as I pulled out a thickly wrapped envelope. "He must have put the shelf in when he was painting the doghouse. I'm willing to bet that Ellen told him to tear it down, and he knew that if he did that, he'd lose his perfect hiding place. So he bought himself some time by sprucing it up."

"Are you saying that these files were never in the locker to begin with? Why did he have the key, then?"

"Maybe he kept moving things around so he wouldn't get caught," I said. "We can't exactly ask him now, can we?"

As I tore away the protective wrapping, I could see all four sets of files inside. A quick glance showed us that they belonged to Heather, Rose, Martha, and a name I didn't recognize. Perhaps she'd been the one who'd paid Morgan off. If I were still investigating Morgan's murder, she'd be at the top of my list, but I still believed that Ellen was guilty.

And when I heard that voice behind us, I knew that I'd been right, no matter how little satisfaction it would give me if Grace and I ended up dead.

After grabbing the files from me and quickly glancing at them, Ellen said, "I kept wondering why he cared so much about that stupid doghouse. I should have found these myself. I told him to tear that thing down, and that idiot brother of mine fixed it up instead."

"You found a few other files yourself, though, didn't you?" I asked.

"Three were in the bus station locker," Ellen admitted as she pointed her gun at us. "I never dreamed that he'd split them up."

"When did you discover what he was doing?" I asked her, trying to buy Grace and me as much time as I could.

"There's no time to talk about that now," Ellen said as she looked around her neighborhood. "Get in the house."

"I'm willing to bet my life that you won't take a chance shooting us outside," I said as I pulled Grace toward her car.

"I said 'move!'" she barked out, and then I heard the shot. It hit eight inches from my foot, and I knew that we were dealing with a maniac.

Suddenly, I had no problem believing that she'd shoot us where we stood.

I looked around as Grace and I took our first steps toward the house. "One of your neighbors might be watching," my best friend said. "That shot was pretty loud, too."

"Everyone who lives around here is at work right now," she said. "That's what I like about this neighborhood. Nobody's going to save you."

"Then why should we go inside at all?" Grace asked. I would have been happier if she hadn't raised that particular question, but Ellen had an answer for her.

"If you want me to shoot you out here and drag you both inside, I'm happy to oblige you. If you go inside, I'll make sure that the shots are clean hits."

Was that supposed to be a real incentive? "Just tell us why you killed Morgan," I asked. "At least give us that before you kill us."

I could tell that Ellen wanted *someone* to know what had really happened. She stopped urging us forward as she said, "As a matter of fact, it was an accident. I discovered that some of my files were missing, and I followed Morgan to April Springs to see what he was up to. When I confronted him about what he was doing, he actually laughed at me. I shoved him, and he had the nerve to shove me back. I wasn't about to take that, so I swung at him one more time. It knocked him back, and he lost his footing. He hit his head hard on the concrete, and the next thing I knew, he was gone." She cried softly as she spoke, and I could see the pain on her face. I knew that didn't mean that she wouldn't shoot us in cold blood, though.

"Why didn't you call the paramedics?" Grace asked. "They might have been able to save him."

"I've had all of the training that they had," she said, dismissing us briskly. "No one could have saved him."

"Someone else is going to figure out what you did," I said. "After all, we did."

"Suspecting and proving are two different things," she

said. "Once you two are gone, I'm willing to take my chances."

"I've heard enough," Chief Martin said as he stepped out from behind the house. "Put down your weapon, Officer."

Ellen started to turn her weapon toward him when another voice barked out from the other side, "Do it now. You can't get both of us."

She looked daunted to learn that her boss was there as well. "Chief, I caught these two breaking into my house."

"Save it for your lawyer," he said. "For now, drop your weapon. This is your last warning, Officer. We *will* shoot."

I cringed, knowing that Grace and I were directly in the line of fire.

If this was going to turn into a shootout, we were in serious trouble.

I saw Ellen's grip on the gun tense for a split second, and I was ready to pull Grace to the ground when the shooting started, but all of a sudden, I could see Ellen's hand slacken, and the handgun tumbled harmlessly onto the ground.

The rest of it was routine for the pair of police chiefs, but Grace and I didn't stop shaking until hours later.

Chapter 20

It felt as though I was interviewed for days instead of hours, and I was hoarse by the time Chief Martin told me that I could go. I wasn't headed anywhere until I found Grace, though, but I still had one more surprise headed my way.

I never expected Jake to be waiting on me.

"I'm so happy that you're here," I said as I hugged him longer than I ever had in my life. "How did you manage it?"

"I was on my way back while you were being interviewed," he said. "Nobody would let me see you. As a cop, I know that it's just protocol, but I was ready to start tearing walls down when you came through."

"Does that mean that you caught the bomber?" I asked him as I pulled away.

"I never got within twenty miles of him. Another team traced the components he used in the device and they arrested him in his apartment. They say that he cried like a baby when they broke in and threw him to the floor. I wish I'd been there, but the only thing that really counted was that he was caught."

"That's wonderful news," I said as I squeezed him again.

Grace came out of another interrogation room. She looked beaten down, and I was sorry that there was no one there to comfort her as well.

No one but me, anyway.

I broke free from Jake's embrace and wrapped Grace up in my arms.

"I can't tell you how glad I am that it's finally over," she said, nearly sobbing from the strain of what we'd just gone through.

"We made it, though, didn't we?"

"We did," she said. "Can we go home now?"

"You'd better believe it," I said as Jake walked toward us

both.

"Hey, I see that you made it back," Grace said to him with a smile.

"A day late and a dollar short, but I'm finally here."

"That's all that counts," she said, and I couldn't agree with her more.

Our world had gone through quite an upheaval in the past few days, and I for one was ready to get back to my quiet life of making donuts and spending time with the people I loved.

It was more than I ever could have asked for.

I wanted to believe Ellen Briar's story that her brother's death had been an accident. After all, she'd lost her family, two brothers lost years apart, and she would most likely spend the rest of her life in prison, alone.

I was never more grateful for my family than I was right then, and I promised myself to give my mother a bone-crushing hug the next time that I saw her.

Just knowing that she was there, and always on my side whether I was right or wrong, was enough for me.

CPSIA information can be obtained at www.ICGtesting.com
Printed in the USA
LVOW13s1711300913

354763LV00003B/535/P